THE DEADLY COACHING INN
Abigail Summers Cozy Mysteries
Book 7

ANN PARKER

Copyright © 2025 Ann Parker

Layout design and Copyright © 2025 by Next Chapter

Published 2025 by Next Chapter

Cover art by Lordan June Pinote

This book is a work of fiction. Names, characters, places, and incidents are the product of the author's imagination or are used fictitiously. Any resemblance to actual events, locales, or persons, living or dead, is purely coincidental.

All rights reserved. No part of this book may be reproduced or transmitted in any form or by any means, electronic or mechanical, including photocopying, recording, or by any information storage and retrieval system, without the author's permission.

Also by Ann Parker

The Deadly Detective Agency
The Deadly Pub Quiz
The Deadly Regatta
The Deadly Fun Run
The Deadly Wedding
The Deadly Museum

*Dedicated to my husband, Terry.
His vast knowledge of all things paranormal
and historical facts made this book possible.*

PARANORMAL WEEKEND AT
THE THREE CROWS IN GRIMBLES CROSS.

Join us for a nighttime vigil at the most
haunted pub on the Chiltern Hills.
Meet celebrity psychic medium, Damien Shadow,
and enter the infamous Room 6 if you dare!
Saturday 9 pm to Sunday 10 am
BOOK NOW

Contact Luke King of
SpooKing Events

Chapter 1

Police Constable Tom Bennett rubbed his hands together as he stood outside Room six of The Three Crows. The corridor was narrow and the uneven walls were starting to make him feel claustrophobic. It seemed very dark for eleven o'clock in the morning, not helped by the small lattice window, warped with age. There was a chill in the air which reminded him that he was in the most haunted building in the Chiltern Hills, according to the locals. They obviously didn't know about the house in Church Lane, Becklesfield, where he lived with his wife, Hayley—or Hayley Moon, to followers of the paranormal.

Tom couldn't help thinking that Hayley would have been a much better celebrity than this Damien Shadow off the television. Then again, Hayley was quite happy helping people and the police while staying out of the public eye.

The young, handsome policeman was used to ghosts, but there was definitely something spooky—perhaps even evil—about this old coaching inn. It was made worse by the dead body he was guarding just six feet away. The forensic team was due, and Tom wished they would hurry up. He peered into the room to look at the body on the bed. The man was sitting up and leaning against the headboard. He could have been thought to have nodded off if it weren't for the fact that he had been stabbed in the chest. The first thing Tom had done when he got to the scene was phone his boss, Detective Chief Inspector Tony Johnson of Gorebridge CID. Then he had phoned his wife.

Hayley and the team—if you could call five spirits a team—were on their way. Hayley had been quite happy doing a few readings and talks for the Women's Institute until dressmaker Abigail Summers had been murdered and, with his wife's help, the case had been solved. After that, they formed The Deadly Detective Agency and assisted the police with their murders—not that the police knew for sure. Hayley would have to stay outside the pub, out of Johnson's way, but he knew Abigail would soon be there sticking her nose in—or as she called it, investigating. Not that Tom could see her, but she still tended to complicate things for him if he had to pass on any observations she had.

Tom was pleased when he heard footsteps coming up the staircase to the first floor and saw Bob and the others with their equipment and cameras.

"Morning, Tom. Nice old pub, isn't it? Full of history."

"Full of something; ghosts, they reckon."

"You a believer, are you? Mind you, I suppose you have to be with your wife."

"You stand here for five minutes on your own and you'll be a believer," snapped Tom.

"Fair enough. Right, who have we got?"

"One of the ghost hunters, Tyler Drayton."

"Well, he's one himself now. What's the murder weapon? Looks like it's made of brass."

"The landlady said it's the toasting fork that's always hanging by the fireplace in the bar. It's been there for years."

"So he's toast," laughed Bob.

Tom rolled his eyes. "I suppose someone had to say it.

Apparently, he had a camera filming to catch any ghosts that might appear, but I couldn't see one. Can you have a good look for it?"

"That'll be handy if there is, and we can get off home. Johnson will be pleased."

"You're joking, Bob. A murder in a pub? He'll be trying to drag it out for days."

"I hadn't thought of that. We'd better get going. Dr Malik is on her way. Let's hope it's all caught on camera."

Chapter 2

Hayley Bennett stopped her little red Mini just down the road from The Three Crows in Grimbles Cross. It was at the crossroads on the old London Road that had been busy until the Gorebridge bypass was built.

She saw the police cars with the blue flashing lights and didn't want to get too close. No doubt her nemesis, DCI Johnson, would be arriving soon. Probably much quicker than usual once he realised the scene had beer on tap, thought Hayley. She had been at the swings with her six-month-old baby, Benjamin, when she had received the phone call from Tom, who told her there had been a murder. The rest of the detective agency had been there, and after dropping Benjie at his Nanny Bennett's, she had brought the spirit members, Abigail, Terry and Betty, to see what had happened. Terry Styles told them he used to drink there in the seventies before he died when he was fifty-four.

"It was always packed back then. We played dominoes and darts in the public bar. But you could hardly see the dartboard because of the smoke. Those were the days. I'd have a ploughman's lunch, which was a hunk of crusty bread and butter, a big slice of cheddar cheese and a pickled onion, followed by a pint and a fag."

"Tell me again why you died at fifty?" said Abigail.

"Everybody smoked back then. It's the teenagers I feel sorry for these days. How can they afford it? When I was young, you could buy a packet of five cigarettes for nine pence; that's old pennies. And they didn't ask how old you were either. I bought my first ones at the age of twelve."

"And you sound so proud." Abigail and Terry didn't agree on everything, but they did love each other. She could drive him up the wall, but her pretty face, with her blue eyes and beguiling smile, always won him over. And he could be grumpy himself at times, so they were a good match. "You might have lived till you were ninety-nine, Terry."

"Maybe so. We thought smoking was good for you back then. It wasn't till all the film stars started dying that it made you wonder. Oh well. I still miss it, you know. Shows how addictive they were. Look, there's the gibbet. That's where they'd hang you if you killed someone or stole a sheep. Hard times. And they'd leave you hanging there for days as a deterrent to others. Especially the highwaymen. It was easy pickings for them on this road. If travellers were going north, south, east or west, they'd get them. So they'd leave them dangling till they rotted."

"Yuck. No wonder there were crows about. They're scavengers, aren't they?"

Terry said, "And if you saw three crows sitting on that branch on the oak tree, that meant someone was going to die. So presumably they were there yesterday."

"They used to say there was an evil polkadot in the pub," said Betty.

"You mean like an orb?" said Abigail.

"No, a polkadot. That's a ghost that moves things. It's

German for nosy ghost." Betty was always getting her words and sayings mixed up, but that was part of her charm. "When I was a girl, we were told that if you held your breath and ran round the tree three times, you'd see the ghost of Murdering Megan." Betty was eighty-two when she died a few years ago, and in death as in life, she was game for anything.

"And did she ever appear?" asked Abigail.

"Well no. But when you're ten that doesn't stop you trying, dear."

"So who was Murdering Megan?"

"They didn't exactly say. Only that she was supposed to haunt the pub. They say there's more ghosts than customers. Well, when I was alive."

"Told you. That's because they stopped the smoking," Terry told them.

"We'll agree to disagree on that, hun," said Hayley, looking at her phone. "Here it is: The Three Crows in the small hamlet of Grimbles Cross. The Three Crows is an old coaching inn that was built in 1574. Travellers could change horses or stay for the night on their way to or from London. It is said that King Charles I spent the night there. It is reputed to be one of the most haunted buildings in England."

Betty looked puzzled. "Did you say Hamlet stayed here? That seems like an awfully long way from Denmark, dear."

"No, hun. A hamlet is a small village without a church. But I wouldn't be surprised if Shakespeare himself had stayed here on his way to and from Stratford-upon-Avon. But luckily for us, you can go and ask all these ghosts that are apparently there."

"This is going to be the easiest case ever," said Abigail. "I don't know whether to be pleased or not. All we have to do is ask the ghosts who it was. If there was a murder in the library, we'd know."

When Abigail Summers herself had been murdered, she met the handsome Terry, who had taken her to the Becklesfield

Public Library where all the spirits would congregate, and where they started to run the agency from once they solved her case. She guessed that it was a lot more peaceful than a busy public house.

Terry said, "But even if they do tell us and we pass it on to Tom, we still have to work out the why and how. And get the evidence to prove it. I'm guessing some of the poor people hanged over there didn't all get a fair trial. Look, there's the old wooden stocks on the green. At least a rotten tomato wasn't fatal. I can think of a few people I'd like to put their hands and feet in."

"You might have been put in there yourself, dear. It was mainly for things like being drunk and disorderly."

"I can assure you, Betty, I have never been disorderly," Terry told her.

Abigail added, "Talking of people I'd like to throw eggs at, I wonder if Johnson is here yet."

"I just saw Dr Malik go in," said Hayley. "Oh, talk of the devil, here he is now."

The dishevelled and cantankerous detective got out of a car that was being driven by his sergeant. His grey hair grew so fast, it always looked like it needed cutting. He put his hands in the pockets of his shiny grey suit and looked at the ancient, white and black-beamed pub from the Tudor days.

"This is a first; a pub I've never been to."

"Impressive, isn't it, sir?" said the young, good-looking Dave Mills.

Johnson looked at the sign Real Ale Served *Here* and said, "I've never seen anything so beautiful in my life, son. Let's find the landlord. I'm sure he'll stand us a pint or two. He'll want this cleared up as soon as possible."

"She, actually, sir. Two ladies run it; the Lockharts, two sisters."

"Really? Oh well, I'm sure they'll be just as hospitable."

"Sir, maybe don't be so... er."

"What are you trying to say, Sergeant? I always treat ladies with the greatest respect. I will today anyway."

Mills thought he'd believe it when he saw it. He was never polite to women. But then he was never polite to anyone. They walked through the arch that led to where the stables once were. The cobblestones were uneven after centuries of being worn by horses' hooves and the wheels of carriages. The two policemen went in through a small door, and Mills had to bow his head to go in, unlike his boss.

Johnson's eyes lit up as he saw a line of beer pumps on the dark oak bar. He ignored the impressive sight of the fireplace, the black beams across the ceiling and down the walls, which were bedecked with souvenirs from all down the centuries.

Two women in their forties were by the bar. One behind and one on a stool, who stood up to greet them.

"Are you the detectives from Gorebridge? I'm Emma and this is Louise."

"My sergeant tells me you're sisters. Is that right? I thought maybe you were both...," to which Mills inwardly groaned.

"No," said Louise, "You wouldn't be the first one to say that. I for one have had my heart broken in a million pieces by a man, Cameron, if you don't believe me. So I've been off men for the last few years, but not for that reason I can assure you."

"How long have you had the pub?"

"About two years, so we haven't had time for dating since then anyway. Can I get you a cup of tea or coffee? I know you're not allowed to drink on duty."

Not the best start, thought Mills. But Johnson didn't seem to mind.

"That's just on the telly, miss. I'll have a pint of your best draught bitter and my sergeant will have an orange juice. He's driving. It would be rude not to sample what's on offer."

Louise took a glass from above her head. "The local brew, Grimble Goblin, is our bestseller."

"Sounds good."

She smiled and said, "Best in the county. Take a seat and I'll bring them over."

As the four of them sat down at one of the tables, Abigail, Terry and Betty joined them. Terry told them it hadn't changed one bit since he'd been there fifty years ago, apart from the new seat covers and maybe the carpet. He stood in front of the bar's centrepiece, the huge brick fireplace. It was laid with logs and newspaper, ready to light when the days grew cold. Next to the black grate, a cast-iron pot was hanging. Down each side were horse brasses on their original leather straps. He didn't notice that a hook on the dark oak surround was now empty, where a seventeenth-century brass toasting fork had once hung. Abigail, who liked symmetry, did notice that something should have been hanging there to balance out the bellows that were on the other side. As Terry was reminiscing about winning first prize in a dominoes contest, he was brought back to the present as Emma started telling the detectives about the paranormal event that was going on at the time of the murder.

Johnson blew out his cheeks. "God help us, Mills. As if I don't have enough trouble with that Hayley Bennett. Now the place is full of them." He took a sip of his beer. "Heaven and hell at the same time. Carry on, love."

"We're not always as busy as we'd like to be, so sometimes we hold ghost-hunting weekends. They pay to stay here and call out to the ghosts. It's always very popular. Although we didn't have many come this time, which is surprising, as we had a celebrity guest. It's run by Luke King and his son – SpooKing Events. We close the hotel for the Saturday night and they have the run of the place."

"So people pay? What do they get for their cash?"

"A room of their choice to sleep in, if they can. But before that, anyone can go and investigate in any of the rooms. There's the cellar and the attic as well. Room six is always in demand as it's got the most activity after all the deaths. And I'm guessing it'll be even more popular now that there's been another murder in there. We can charge double now."

"And they actually see ghosts, do they?"

"Not exactly, Inspector. But they've got all sorts of equipment these days. You don't need to see them with your own eyes."

"In my day it was an upturned glass and bits of paper."

"They still do that. But now they video and record everything, which I should think will be very handy for your investigation."

"If not, we'll communicate with them and just ask. So did you know the murdered man?"

Louise answered first, "I'd heard of him. He's called Tyler Drayton."

Emma added, "He's got the YouTube channel – The Daring Draytons. He does it with his wife."

"Okay, so I'll need to have a word with her first."

"Ah, that's the trouble, Inspector; she's missing."

"Now I'm told," said Johnson, staring hard at Mills.

"I haven't had a chance to talk to anyone yet, sir. So what's her name?" he asked and got out his notebook.

"Rachel. We saw her last night. When they first come we get them in here and serve them drinks. They all have a chat and say what they're going to do, and Luke and his son, Calum, tell them the history of the place. We close the bar at eleven and leave them to it," said Emma.

"Where do you two go when all this is happening?"

"We've got our rooms on the second floor. They know not to go in there and we lock the door anyway at the top of the stairs. The small staircase further along is open as that goes up to the attic. Mind you, I wouldn't go in there at night. I've not seen anything myself but that is definitely haunted. I was shattered by then, so I just put on my dressing gown and read my book. I didn't hear anything unusual, did you, Louise?"

"Nothing. Running a pub is hard work, Inspector. We sleep well. But if you want to know about Rachel you'd better ask Luke King, he's worked with her a lot."

Mills wanted to know who the celebrity guest was.

"Damien Shadow. Have you heard of him? Well, I suppose you have to be interested in the supernatural. He used to be on TV a lot. Not so much now. You'll know which one he is when you see him," laughed Emma.

"How did you find out about the murder?"

"We came down at about nine to make them coffee and nothing seemed wrong. We chatted to them in the bar for a while. But when no one had seen the Draytons, Luke went to look and said he'd been knocking to wake the dead, so he went in. I couldn't believe it at first," said Emma. "He looked dead but I still felt for a pulse. But his wrist was stone cold, so it was obvious he'd gone. The colour wasn't right and his head was resting on his chest. I don't think I'll ever get the picture out of my mind."

"It must have been a shock for you, miss. Could you see how he'd been killed?"

"I'm guessing it was by our antique toasting fork that was sticking out of his chest. You can see where it should have been over there."

"A toasting fork, that's a new one, Mills. So don't touch anything. The team will be down to look for prints, et cetera. Where is everyone that was here?"

"In the other bar. And our star is not happy at being kept here. The others don't mind at all. They're still trying to make contact with the other side."

"Mr Shadow will have to wait. I've got to go up and talk to the doctor first."

"Would it be all right if we went upstairs?" asked Louise. "We really need to cancel the customers who have booked for Sunday lunch and those who've booked rooms."

"Of course. But before you go, I need to have another pint of your excellent Grimble Goblin."

Chapter 3

ABIGAIL, TERRY AND BETTY HAD BEEN VERY interested in what the two sisters had told the police. And so were the four resident and infamous ghosts of the old pub.

Terry introduced his companions and asked if they would mind if they stayed.

"Not at all," said the lady dressed in her nightgown. "I'm Megan. Or Murdering Megan as I get called now. Not that I mind. It makes me sound a lot more exciting, and it means I'm not likely to be forgotten."

"So why do they call you that then?" asked the nosy Abigail. "Were you a murderer?"

"Not even that. I died of old age in me bed at the ripe old age of fifty-three. I was the barmaid and general dogsbody here. Don't ask me when."

"You were already here when I died," said a shifty-looking man with red hair, who you wouldn't want to meet in a dark alley, thought Betty. "That was 1850, give or take. I'm Morton Glasspool. And this is our young stable lad, Timmy Scarlet."

A monk in a brown habit with his hood partially covering his face said, "Friar Oswyn. Pleased to meet you all."

"That's a nasty-looking gash you have there, Oswyn," said Terry, wincing.

"A sword, sir. They were hard times to be a monk."

"I remember learning about it at school. Don't worry, King Henry is not talked of fondly these days."

"I'm glad to hear it."

"He had two of his own wives beheaded, you know."

"Did he really? The man was the very devil."

Abigail never was one for small talk. "I'm so sorry, but we're actually here to investigate the death of the man who was killed upstairs last night. I expect you know exactly who did it. Just give us the name or point them out and we'll take it from there."

The four ghosts looked at each other. The scruffy-looking man spoke first. "How would we know? It wasn't one of us."

"We didn't say it was. But surely you were here. It was a ghost weekend. You must have a great time at those."

Megan rolled her eyes. "The first ones, yes. And some of them are really good. They know exactly where we are and we always try to get through to them if we can. Timmy can touch things if he really concentrates. Like last night, they had a glass and he spelt out his name. But the trouble is, none of us can spell nowt but our names. Morton has got his smell, but that's about it."

"I don't know why they say they can smell something awful when I goes near 'em. I died in the summer and I'd only had a bath in the spring. So we just stay for an hour or two to give them a bit of fun and then go and see our friends in the village hall."

"It's true," said Oswyn. "The so-called ghost hunters say, 'Is there anybody there? Show yourself'. And when we do, they don't see a thing. Either that or they scream."

Timmy added, "And they have these magic boxes these days

that have all these noises come out of them. Would give me an 'eadache if I could still get one."

"Although one of them could see something. I'd not seen him before. A man in a fancy outfit. But we still left. And sometimes they try to send us to the light by burning something and waving it about. But we'll go when we're ready, thank you very much," said Megan.

"Another one said he saw a shadow figure right by where I was standing," said Morton. "But we still left them to it. Sorry about that. What's it got to do with you anyway? Do you know the poor man?"

Betty said proudly, "No. You could say we wrong rights. Or is it right wrongs? One of the three anyway. Abigail started a detective agency when she was murdered herself. And now we help the police."

"Very honourable, miss."

"So when did you get back from the village hall?" asked Abigail.

"I don't know times," said Megan, "but everyone was running around like headless chickens. We followed the noise and saw him dead on the bed. Last time I saw him he was knocking back the whiskies and his wife was nagging him to stop. And she's gone missing."

"So you don't know anything," said Abigail miserably.

"We know where the other body is though," said Morton.

That cheered Abigail up. She knew that Hayley could tell Tom and they would beat the real detectives. It had to be the wife if she was missing.

"Where is it?" she asked excitedly.

"In the cellar. In a barrel."

"Can you excuse me for a minute," said Abigail as she ran off to tell Hayley, leaving Terry and Betty to explain who Hayley was.

"So you think the wife's body is in this barrel," said Hayley. "I guess I'd better let Tom know. Poor Tom. We do drop him in it."

When poor Tom got the text message he was still outside the room while his boss was talking to Dr Malik. All it said was, 'Body in barrel in cellar. Maybe the wife. Tell Johnson'. It was going to need thinking about. Tom could never work out why Johnson didn't want Hayley's help. She'd closed most of his cases whether he liked it or not; and he usually didn't. Tom decided to wait a while and listen to what the doctor said so he could pass it on.

"Male in his forties. Full rigor mortis."

"So you think he was stabbed to death quite a few hours ago, Doctor?"

"I'd say roughly between 4 am and 6 am. I won't know for sure until I've done the proper tests. Punctured his left lung. Death wouldn't have been instantaneous, I'm afraid. So he may have had the chance to call out, although I daresay he was struggling for breath. No prints on the top end of the murder weapon, so it would have been wiped unless they were wearing gloves."

She held up a large evidence bag. Inside was an ornate brass toasting fork. The four-inch prongs were stained with blood and very sharp.

"Forensics found the victim's fingerprints on this end. Whether he was trying to pull it out we can only imagine. A dreadful way to go, Inspector."

"Indeed. It would take a lot of force to push that in, I reckon."

"And the fact that he's sitting up would make it harder. With the length of the implement I doubt I'll find any DNA of the killer on his hands or nails."

Johnson added, "Hmm, you're right. I daresay he or she had it down by the side of them and attacked him before he knew what was happening."

"I was told there's no sign of the wife. If she was here they weren't under the covers."

"They weren't here for any hanky-panky, Doctor. Trying to raise the dead. I wonder why I'm thinking of my second wife in the bedroom?" sighed Johnson.

Even the doctor had to smile at that. "So I heard. Not about your wife; about communicating with the dead. This is where Murdering Megan is supposed to have killed her victims."

"Mills, put out an APB for one Murdering Megan, aged a hundred years. In fact, get that Moon woman to bring her in for questioning."

"Do you mean Hayley Moon? Isn't she wonderful?" said the doctor cheerfully.

"No she's not," snapped Johnson. "I think it's more likely to be the wife. What do I say, Mills? It's always the wife."

The doctor added with a smile, "I can see why it would be in your case, Tony."

"She's softening, Mills. She called me Tony. So I want that wife, Rachel Drayton, found. She's either guilty or another victim."

Tom was starting to sweat. Why did he have a wife that put him in these impossible situations? But he did love her to death. And she would be the death of him one day. He took a deep breath and entered the bedroom.

"Do you want me to do a search for her, sir? There's a few uniforms here now."

"Good idea, lad. You're only standing there doing nowt. Get WPC Jane Nichols to do a door-to-door."

Tom ran down the creaky staircase to find the others. He split them into pairs and found Louise Lockhart to ask her to show him and PC Coult where the cellar was. He put on his gloves and lifted the latch on the studded oak door. Louise told him there was a pull cord for the light and as soon as he put his hand in he felt the temperature drop. The creaking door and the perilously steep stairs didn't put his mind at rest either. Even all the ghosts who followed them could feel the tension in the air.

"There's nothing down here, Constable. I've already looked. I think I would have noticed if Mrs Drayton was in here, dead or alive," said Louise.

"We have to check everywhere. Even the barrels."

"The only barrels here are the ones from the local brewery. Two are still full and those ones are waiting to be picked up."

Tom lifted up the empty ones and looked around. The concrete floor was well swept but there was a desolate look to the place. There were crates of beer and wine on one wall and nowhere a body could be hidden. He was about to give up when he received another text from Hayley.

"Miss Lockhart, what's behind this shelving unit?"

"Nothing. The wall, I presume," she answered, looking confused.

"Constable, help me move it."

After rocking it from side to side, it moved and they could see an alcove behind it. Tom knew right away that the barrel that was there could not have contained the body of the wife. It was covered in grime and dust from years of decay. He tried to move the thick cobwebs which criss-crossed the lid, but they kept sticking to his gloves and he couldn't shake them off. Eventually, he cleared the top and gently lifted it and peered inside.

Tom immediately jumped back involuntarily. A skull, with its jaw dropped, was topped with sparse red hair. The man had a faded green shirt and his knees, which were on his chest, showed that he was wearing brown tweed trousers. A strip of dark red material was around his throat.

"Stand back, please. It's a body, just not the one we thought."

Abigail and Terry turned slowly to the man standing at the bottom of the stairs.

Going by the hair and the bright red kerchief tied around his neck, they were looking at the body of Morton Glasspool. Abigail crossed her arms and gave him one of her looks that no one liked to get.

"Is there something you want to tell us?"

"Before you say anything, Miss Abigail, do you know how long I've waited for someone to find me? And to know that you'll be stuffed in there for eternity?"

"You're right, I'd hate it, Morton. Don't worry, we're not judging. I don't blame you at all. You should have seen the fuss I made when I was first dead."

"Oh, she did," agreed Betty. "She was a right pain in the whatsit. You'd think no one had…"

"Thank you, Betty. Do you know who did it?"

"I do, miss. The landlord, William Gillies. We were playing cards late one night. He'd lost big and had to put up every penny he had. I'd never been so lucky, so I thought. Then he wagered the inn and lost. I was never going to get out alive after that. His mate Jim was playing as well and I'd cleared him out too. Gillies strangled me with this," he said, pointing to his neck.

"Did he get caught?" asked Terry. "Hopefully you got to see him swinging on the gallows."

"Nah. I waited every day hoping they'd end up on the noose but they never did. Me wife thought I'd left her and the bairns and she wasn't sorry. The six youngsters missed me, but I hadn't been there for them much, I soon realised. Drinking and cards. She always said they would be the death of me."

"At least you can have a proper burial now. Our friend Hayley can make sure of that. They'll have to take the bones to look at them but then you can rest in peace. I bet there are even some next of kin who could go to the burial."

"There are a few Glasspools still in the village. I guess I'll go and join the wife after. Say I'm sorry at last."

"That's lovely, dear. I'll be joining my John one day. When we've caught a few more killers."

"Which we won't if we don't get on," said Abigail. "But where is the victim's wife then? Did she snap and kill him? Or was she a witness who had to die? She could be anywhere. I suppose we'll have to leave it to the police to find her."

Friar Oswyn stepped out of a dark corner. "Then again, she might be in the priest hole."

Chapter 4

DCI JOHNSON WAS NOT IMPRESSED AT ALL THAT PC Bennett had found a body in the cellar. But he did laugh when he was told that it could have been there for a hundred years or more.

He told Mills as they went down the steep stairs to look, "All he's done is made more expense for the budget. The Chief Constable won't be happy."

"Bit spooky, isn't it, sir? I wouldn't want to be on my own down here like that lot did. And they were in the dark with just a night-vision light."

"More fool them. Can't believe they'd pay good money to wander around a pub that's not even serving."

"I'd love to do it. It must be exciting. Don't think the wife would agree to go though."

"Okay, Mills, we'd better take a look at the John Doe. I wonder if there was beer in there. Worse ways to go, I suppose."

"Hopefully he was dead before he was put in there, sir. Do you think there's any connection to the body upstairs?"

"No, nothing at all. It was hidden, wasn't it? God knows how Bennett found it. Mind you, they might both be victims of

Murdering Megan. No, Sergeant, I reckon Drayton's wife got fed up with spending her weekends filming ghosts and lost it."

"But it must have been planned. Someone went into the bar and took the weapon upstairs. Surely if it had been on impulse she would have picked up the lamp. Or even her torch. There was a large one on the side."

"Ahem, I was wondering when you would work that out, son. Cor blimey, that's a sight, isn't it? They must have been smaller in those days. It's enough to put you off your beer. I wonder who he was. Don't suppose we'll ever find out. Come on, I'm beginning to get the heebie-jeebies myself. Let's go and interview these ghostbusters."

Tom was standing at the top of the stairs. "What do you think, sir?"

"I think you've found nothing but a lot of work. Better get Bob back to dust for prints. There'll definitely be a lot of dust, not sure about the prints. And I'm guessing we won't be able to get a conviction. So where are the likely ones for the real murder?"

Tom took out his notes. "They're all in the bar. There's a celebrity here, sir – Damien Shadow and his cameraman, Scott Clarkson. The pair that organised it – Luke and Calum King, father and son. And the ones who paid to come are Julia Guildford, Mia Beckett, Peter Peacock and Grant Mayfair. And obviously the Draytons."

"Let's get it over with then. Might be able to have another pint before we go back to the station then, Mills. While we question young Louise behind the bar of course."

As the three of them entered, a man jumped to his feet. Going by his purple suit, flamboyant long hair and the large gold crucifix around his neck, Johnson guessed that he was the celebrity medium, Damien Shadow.

"At last, Inspector, I've been kept here for hours. And I don't know anything about the attack on this man. Scott was filming me for the entire time so he can vouch for me. Then after we'd finished I was in my room in the converted stable block on my own. Apart from a young stable boy actually."

"What you get up to is your own affair, sir. But I will need his details."

"Really, Inspector. I'm a married man and don't mean that at all. The stable boy was from the other side. A ghost, if you will. Deceased."

"Not going to be a very good alibi then, is he? And you're not impressing me. I know a psychic that would knock your fancy socks off," Johnson said, looking back at Tom.

"Thank you, sir. I don't think I've ever heard you say anything nice about my wife."

"You probably won't again, so make the most of it."

"So can I go? I'm quite prepared to give you my address. I've got an interview to do later today, and I'm going to have a Zoom meeting from my hotel room."

"You can have as quick a one as you like, you're not going anywhere till you've given your statement to one of the constables. So did any of you know the deceased man?"

"I don't know any of these people," said Damien. "Mr King booked me over the phone."

"So sit down and be quiet then."

Luke King looked around. "That's me; I booked him. I'm a demon hunter."

"Then we have something in common," said Johnson. "That's what I do."

Luke carried on, "We all knew Tyler. He'd been to a lot of these."

Scott said, "I filmed a few of these events with different clients so I knew him. But he used his wife to film him. He would say hi, but that was about it."

The two young girls denied it. "We didn't know him at all. We only came for a laugh."

"And was it?" Mills said to Julia and Mia.

"It was to start with. But he kept telling us to shut up." Mia pointed to Damien Shadow. "Then we got a bit scared. Especially when we went up to the attic."

"We're never coming again," added Julia. "But the murder was cool. We thought it was part of the weekend until the police got here. You know, like a mystery game."

"Did you two go in Room six?"

"We went in with Damien. That's when he told us to be quiet. And we were getting bored and tired by then. So we went back to our room in the stable block and watched a film till we fell asleep," said Mia.

"Mills, take them next door to give a statement and they can go." Johnson ignored Damien's protestations.

Peter Peacock, a young man in a grey hoodie and glasses, admitted to knowing the Draytons. "I met them at the Courtridge Hotel a couple of times. They started running paranormal days there earlier this year."

That was down to Hayley, Tom thought. Hayley and the ghosts had solved a murder after she had seen the ghost of a teenager in the grounds. He had been buried there, and after that the owners took Hayley's advice and held their own ghost hunts and paranormal weekends.

"What about you?" Johnson pointed to a bearded young man. He had a T-shirt that read GPS. Grant Mayfair explained that it stood for the Gorebridge Paranormal Society.

"The Draytons have a YouTube channel called the Daring Draytons. 'They dare so you don't have to', so they say. They've got over two hundred thousand followers. They had me on once and I interviewed them on my podcast. But I wouldn't say I know anything about them. We did notice that they didn't get on very well. They were snapping at each other last night. We think it was her and she ran off."

"Did any of you see her leave? What about you, Mr Shadow? Your room is near the car park."

"I heard a car pull away at about four during the night. But I don't know if it was her."

"Bennett, I never thought of that. Is their car still here? If it's gone, we'll know it's her."

"It's still outside, sir."

"Shame. So what happens on these things? Do you all stay together? Give us a rough idea."

Luke told him, "We started off with welcoming drinks in the bar, then we turned the lights down to a minimum to get us in the mood. We started off like we always do with a spirit board. We heard some knocking and the glass came up with the name Timmy. We didn't get any more, so we split up. The two girls walked about and then went to the attic. Rachel and Tyler stayed together. She does the filming and he calls out. The camera! You'll have a recording of whoever did it, Inspector. He would have had one going in the room."

"Unfortunately there wasn't a camera in there."

"There you are then," said Damien. "His wife must have taken it with her."

"Or any of you. Mills, make sure all their rooms are searched. So you split up and went into all the different rooms. Did you find any ghosts? Perhaps you could ask them who did it."

Peter Peacock got very serious. "It doesn't work like that. Although I did feel something touch my back in the courtyard and from time to time I could smell something disgusting. Look, this is a spirit box. It picks up static and records the spirits. I actually got a lot of communication early last night. I'm an empath, so I feel when a ghost is there rather than see them. But it trailed off during the night."

Grant said, "You're right, Pete, my EMF meter was going off

the charts and I saw something on the laser grid right after the spirit pod lit up."

Johnson was finding it hard to keep up. Especially when young Peter said, "My cat's balls were going off like mad."

"Hang on a minute. You brought a cat here?"

That made them all laugh, which didn't please Johnson at all.

"No. They were originally toys for cats. But now we buy them. If a spirit comes near them, they light up and start flashing. I put some on the floor in the cellar and on the stairs and they kept going off. And I'm not surprised. I felt like there was something going on in there. I almost had a panic attack. I actually had to leave because I was finding it hard to breathe. There was something in there that didn't want to be there. I put my hand on a wall and felt someone's soul. And I don't think I've ever felt so cold," said Peter with a shiver.

"Then I'm guessing that you're going to be very pleased to hear that we found another body in there."

They all started talking between themselves, so Mills had to tell them to be quiet.

"It was behind a shelf and had been there for a long time," said Johnson. "I daresay you'll hear all about it on the news later. But I'm more interested in the chap upstairs. What about you?" he asked the bearded Grant.

"I got some good footage in the attic. A loud bang and there was no one else there. I think I was there at about two o'clock. The Draytons were coming out as I went in. I didn't talk to them but I heard him say they should go outside by the stable block. There's a young boy that's been seen there. And sometimes the sound of a carriage has been heard going past. I think that was the last time I saw them."

"Are there any of you who have got a confirmed alibi from three o'clock onwards?"

"I was with Dad till about four and then I went to the attic and then to my room. I was in Room three," said Calum.

"Did you hear anything from the deceased's room?"

"That was opposite. No, nothing. But the walls and doors are very thick in these old buildings. And I was awake till about five. I heard the floorboards creaking a few times. In the corridor and on the stairs. But I assumed it was one of us. It could be someone from outside, couldn't it? Like a maniac."

"Unlikely. The doors were locked. So none of you can think of anyone that would have a reason to kill Mr Drayton. But you all look as guilty as a puppy standing next to a puddle of water. Come on. It's an offence to keep information to yourself."

Damien looked around at the others. "Well I've got nothing to hide, Inspector. While we were in the bar having a drink, or in Drayton's case three or four, he made a comment. He actually said, and it could have been aimed at anyone, 'I know one of you is a cheat. It was at the four-star hotel in Amersford when you cheated. I won't be forgetting.' So, Inspector, I have no idea where that hotel is. And I think I've proven my credentials over the years."

"What about the rest of you? Have you ever done your little ghost thing there?"

"We all have at different times," said Luke. "I've done a couple of events there if he's talking about the Kings Arms."

Peter Peacock said, "But none of us have ever cheated. Well I haven't. I heard my first ghost walking when I was six and saw one a year later. I've been trying to prove it to others ever since. No one believed me and that can hurt you as a child. It still affects me now. So I have no reason to fabricate anything. Grant, you seemed to get a lot of activity at that hotel. Was that the night you had three scratches on your back?"

"What if it was? You're still dining out on the time you were hit in the face by that invisible entity in that old asylum."

"You know damn well…"

"That's enough," said Johnson. "So Mr Drayton didn't say who he was making this accusation against?"

Luke King looked around. "No he didn't. None of us would pretend to get something if we hadn't. But there are some that would, I suppose. It's easy to say you saw something or heard a noise." He turned to face Damien Shadow. "Or say you've been possessed by a serial killer from the seventeenth century."

"What are you saying, King? How dare you. That was in an old jail, Inspector, and it was real, alright. It was how I made my name, and experts have all agreed it was real."

Everybody started having their say on who they thought it was until Johnson shouted, "If you don't shut up I'll have you all thrown in jail! Thank you. I don't care if you've thrown the cat's ball or pretended you've been taken over by Jack the Ripper, I just want to know who killed the man upstairs. And apart from the two girls, no one has got an alibi. Just tell your movements to the constable and make sure we have your names and addresses. And don't leave the area."

"I live in Norwich," said Damien angrily. "I'm staying at the Courtridge Hotel for two nights and then I need to get back to my wife."

"Then you'll have to hope we solve it then, won't you?"

"We won't be going anywhere," said Peter Peacock. "I think I can say for all of us that we want to go home and upload all of our investigations and look for anomalies. Then post it to our fans. This is going to be huge. I got a great orb in the attic."

"And I can say for all of us that Tikbook or your podgrams will have to wait. I want all your cameras, videos, recordings, phones and anything else you used given to my sergeant. No exceptions, Mr Shadow. Then you can go. You'll get receipts, don't worry. As soon as we've made copies you can have them back. Shouldn't be more than a day or so. Don't worry, the ghosts aren't going anywhere."

That was apart from Terry, Abigail and Betty, who went back to the car to tell Hayley all about it.

Chapter 5

"Sorry we were a long time, Hayley," said Abigail. "But we had to see what they all told Johnson. We've got a rough idea of what they were all doing."

"It's so annoying I can't go in there. But never mind, I've been sitting here thinking that they can't stop me going for a drink tomorrow if they're allowed to open. What did you find out?"

Terry couldn't wait to tell her. "There's a priest hole in there somewhere. And Friar Oswyn thinks that Rachel Drayton might be in there. Dead or alive, I suppose."

"That is interesting. Can't they go in and have a look? They must know where it is."

"That's what I said, dear. But he said it's pitch black in there and unless the panel is open they can't see a thing. And they wouldn't be able to feel anything."

"That's true, Betty. Oh, God, I'll have to text Tom again. Did you get to see Damien Shadow? I used to watch him when he was on the telly, but he hasn't been on for ages."

Betty said, "I like him. He's rather gorgeous."

"He always was. Mind you, he must be getting on a bit now."

"But he looks exactly the same, doesn't he, Abigail?"

"He does, actually. I can see why he attracts the ladies, alive and dead."

Terry scoffed. "Rubbish. I reckon he was wearing make-up. He's older than me."

"Aw, Terry's jealous. Don't worry. You're the only man for me."

"And you should see what he's wearing, Hayley," said Betty. "Very fancy."

"A purple suit?"

"How did you guess? Oh yes, you're psychic."

"No. He always wore that suit. And had a mass of thick hair."

"He still has," Abigail told her. "Very sexy."

Terry mumbled, "He looks a bit wiggy to me."

"Rubbish. I'd be able to tell."

Terry told Hayley, "He's no psychic. I'd trust him about as much as an electrician without any eyebrows."

"He's made a good living out of it though. But getting back to the secret room," said Hayley, "why didn't the landladies mention it? They must know it's there. I'm sure I heard about it once."

"Why would a pub have a priest hole anyway?" asked Abigail. "It's not like the monks or priests would be there drinking when the king's men were looking. Wouldn't it be somewhere a bit more religious?"

"But usually there were tunnels running from place to place. There used to be a priory near here, so I reckon it went from there and they could get away by staying in hiding or leaving the inn," said Hayley. "I do hope they don't find the wife in there. That would be horrendous."

Abigail said, "But you're thinking she could be another victim. She could just as easily be the murderer and be in there hiding. They're seasoned ghost hunters, so they might have known of it."

"Or she could have got out the other end of the tunnel, if there is one. Although sometimes it was just a cupboard. Rather her than me. I suppose I'd better mention it to Tom. He's not going to be happy if I tell him. But the trouble is we've got no idea where it is, have we?"

"All Oswyn said was that it's between the fireplace and the bar."

Hayley took out her phone again. "We don't want Johnson to leave before he's checked it out."

"Oh, don't worry about that. He's in his element. While there's any beer left in a barrel he won't be in a hurry," Abigail told her.

After Hayley had messaged Tom and she was left alone, she leant back in her seat. If only she could have been there. Suddenly something caught her eye in her rear-view mirror.

"For God's sake, you scared me to death," said Hayley, trying to get her heart to stop pounding. "Don't do that."

A scary-looking old woman with wild hair was sitting in the back seat. "Have you seen my grandson?"

Hayley blew her cheeks out. "I have no idea. Who is your grandson?"

"I promised to look after him. Now I can't find him. Can you help me?"

"I can try, if you haven't given me a heart attack. When did you last see him?"

"I saw him yesterday, but he never went home. I'm worried something has happened to him."

"I need to ask this: is he in the spirit realm as well, hun?"

"No. He's full of life. I need to know that he's all right. He's a lovely boy. He always came to see me when I was alive. He'd make me a cup of tea and I'd bake him a cake. When he was young, he'd stay with me and we'd stay up till midnight watching all his programmes and eating chocolate and popcorn. Please find him for me."

"I'll try. What's his name?"

"Samuel."

Hayley turned around to find out his surname, but the old lady had already vanished.

Chapter 6

ABIGAIL WAS CORRECT. JOHNSON WAS ENJOYING THE case more than he ever had before. There was free beer and he had a driver. His poor sergeant only wanted to get home to his wife and his little girl. He was determined to get going as soon as he had helped the constables to get the statements.

The DCI was sitting on a bar stool talking to Emma, who was behind the bar. Her sister Louise was sitting at one of the tables on her laptop. She was still trying to rebook the guests who wouldn't be able to come for at least two days.

Tom heard his phone ping as he was taking details from Calum King. He guessed it was Hayley and decided to ignore it. But curiosity won and he sneaked a quick look. The text was short and to the point: 'Priest hole next to the bar and fireplace'. He was tempted to keep quiet. His shift was due to finish soon and he wanted to spend some time with Benjie. And his poor mum had been babysitting all day. Surely they could check it out tomorrow? But then if there was something in there, maybe even the victim's wife, she could be gone by tomorrow—or dead. So he finished with Calum and then approached Mills.

"Don't ask how, but I've had a text from someone who said

there's a priest hole to the right of the fireplace. You know, one of those secret rooms."

Dave could guess who had told him that. Unlike his boss, he was quite happy to get to the top on Tom's coattails. He was looking forward to the day when he was the inspector and Tom was his sergeant.

"That's annoying. I thought we could get off. But it needs checking. The wife might be in there. Okay, I'll tell the boss. Let's hope the owners know where it is. Funny they didn't tell us. A bit suspicious, that. Come on, let's go and have a look."

"Sir, Tom and I were thinking that we seem to remember there was a priest hole in this bar. I'm sure we learned about it at school," lied Mills. "It's over to the right of the fireplace, I think. We should check it before we go, sir."

Johnson didn't feel very happy to hear that either. He was just telling Emma all the beers he'd had over the years in different parts of England. He was talking with more affection than he ever did about his two marriages, Dave thought.

"Do you know anything about one, Miss Lockhart?" asked Dave.

"No. It's the first time I've heard about it. We would have been told, surely. Louise, there isn't a priest hole here, is there?"

"I have no idea. But the inn was about at that sort of time. Don't forget they were used over five hundred years ago, so I suppose it could have just been forgotten about."

"We should look, sir. Mrs Drayton could be in there. Or even the murderer."

"Bit of a stretch, but it wouldn't hurt to look, I suppose. Go on then, lad."

Mills, with the help of Tom, started knocking and pushing on the wooden panels, but nothing moved. Emma told them that the only thing behind there were the ovens in the kitchen. The noise sounded a bit more hollow as they got closer to the fire and lower down, but there was no sign of an opening.

Tom had a quick peek at his phone again. One of the ghosts must have relayed to Hayley that they couldn't find how to get in there.

"Excuse me. I was thinking that sometimes there is a lever or button that opens it."

"Like a candlestick," said Johnson sarcastically. "I looked, there isn't one. Go on then, if you think you can do it."

Tom counted four bricks down from the mantelpiece and felt for a break in the oak surround. A piece about six inches long swivelled towards him and they all heard a click as a small panel swung silently open.

"Well, I never," said Johnson. "I don't even want to know how you did that. But we would have found it in the end. These priests must have been small. Go on then, Bennett, in you go."

"Me? It's dark in there, sir. And there are probably spiders. I think forensics should go first. I don't want to ruin any evidence, do I?"

"Put some gloves on, you'll be fine. Spiders won't hurt you. It's the rats you've got to worry about. I'm joking, you soft lad. Give him a torch, love," he said to Louise. She soon found one and gave it to the reluctant Tom.

"I still think forensics should go in first, sir."

"They're still in the cellar thanks to you. Get a move on, it could be empty for all we know."

Tom put his head in the hole and shone the torch. He pulled back quickly as he remembered what he'd seen in the barrel.

"Go on, boy," said Johnson irritably. "My beer's getting warm. What can you see?"

"Not much. Cobwebs. It's a tiny room, about three feet by three. Only room for one person. Oh, there's a drop over there. Looks like it could be the start of a tunnel. Or maybe it's the end of one. It goes down about four feet. Hang on, I'll shine the torch down."

Tom went silent and they all got excited. Abigail was right there next to him, trying to make out what was down there.

"Well, Bennett? Can you see a body?"

"No, sir. But now we know what happened to the Draytons' camera and recordings. They're in pieces down there."

"Well, don't touch that. Drop down and see where it goes to."

Not likely, thought Tom. "I can't till it's been moved. And I'm not going on my own. It could go anywhere."

But again he was told by Hayley, and he could just read the text, so he said, "I reckon it goes to Grimbles Priory, sir. I'm coming out. I can't breathe."

Tom needed to get out fast. The air in there was stale and he was covered in dust and cobwebs.

"All right. Tape this area off," said Johnson. "Where's the priory?" he asked Emma.

"There's no priory that I know of. But there is a big house called Priory Lodge. That was where it was, I expect. Your best bet is to ask Miss Trippet, who runs the village shop. She's about a hundred and knows all the history of the place. She's written a book about it. But it's shut now."

"We can't do much till tomorrow then. Come on, Mills, you can drive me home and we'll come back in the morning. Maybe one for the road, love."

Abigail, Terry and Betty thanked Oswyn and the others and hurried back to Hayley to tell her what had been found. Then they made their way back through the lanes to Becklesfield to have a meeting of The Deadly Detective Agency.

As they drove past, Terry looked at the ancient tree when he heard cawing, and saw there were three crows sitting on a branch. The crows' black, beady eyes didn't leave his until he was out of sight, as if sending a warning to someone or something.

Chapter 7

By the time Hayley had fetched a sleepy Benjamin from his nanny's, the last two ghostly members of the agency had been told about the murder.

Lillian Yin was a nurse in life and was still in her uniform. She had promised to look after Suzie in death, who was a beautiful black girl who had been knocked down by a drunk driver when she was nine.

As the library had closed for the night and Hayley couldn't join them, they went to her cottage in Church Lane. The one with the dreamcatcher and the wind chimes in the porch. In fact, they were already sitting in her conservatory when she got back.

"Come in," said Hayley with a grin. "Make yourself at home."

Benjie was waving his arms excitedly. All thoughts of getting in his cot were gone. Although he was only six months old, he had inherited his mother's gift for the supernatural. He could see all the spirits as easily as he saw his nanny. And so could Luna, the tortoiseshell cat. Although he never showed any interest in them. He soon learned that they couldn't feed him or serve him in a way he had become accustomed to. In fact, every time one of them came round they either took the lady off somewhere or talked so much that he was ignored completely. He did love the little human one though. Luna hadn't at first. He made too much noise and got too much attention. And he gave off this awful smell sometimes and didn't get moaned at about it like he did. Luckily, if Luna made enough noise and jumped on the kitchen worktop, she fed him. That always worked. Once fed, he settled on Hayley's lap in the conservatory.

"So, have you two been told all about the murder at the inn?"

"Both of them," said Suzie excitedly. "One's solved, I know, but who do you think killed the man on the bed, Abigail?"

"Tyler Drayton, and I think his wife, Rachel, did it. I reckon she knew about the tunnel and left through there. The police will find her."

"And the ghosts don't know?" asked Lillian. "I find that hard to believe."

"They left before it happened. They were helpful, though. They heard the couple arguing at times."

"I used to argue with my John. Doesn't mean I'd stick a toasting fork in him, though. I think it's Damien Shadow. He's very handsome, but he looks a bit shifty to me. Even if he has the most gorgeous blue eyes that you could dive into. And the most beautiful smile."

"I can't wait to see him, Betty," said Lillian. "Are there any other suspects?"

Terry said, "There are, but I don't trust Damien. Bet that's not his real name either. Probably took it off that scary film with Gregory Peck."

Abigail counted the suspects on her fingers. "There were four other ghost hunters: Julia Guildford, her friend Mia, Grant Mayfair, and Peter Peacock. Then the two that ran it: father and son, Luke and Calum King. But they were joining in as well. They all had rooms there. The two girls shared, and so did the Draytons. And the victim accused someone of cheating at a past event. Oh, and the landladies — they're sisters, Emma and Louise Lockhart. They share a flat on the top floor and say they locked themselves in."

"Don't forget the cameraman, Scott," said Betty. "He says he slept like a baby in one of the stable rooms and didn't hear anything. But who knows. If anyone can doctor footage, a cameraman can."

"That's very true, actually."

"What were the ghosts like? You said there was a young boy there," asked Suzie. "How old was he?"

"Older than you, dear. I'd say twelve. Old enough to work as a stable boy. He could do a bit of haunting, but nothing like you."

Suzie was what Terry called a Mover. He thought it was because she was a child. It came in very handy for investigating and searching. And she had even saved Hayley's life in the past.

Terry told her, "The monk is a nice man. A very gentle type. You'd like Megan as well, Suzie. Morton Glasspool is happy that he can be laid to rest now. He's waited all these years to be found. He tried so many times to tell someone, but you're the first medium that's understood, Hayley."

"I'm going to the pub to talk to them as soon as it opens again. He might want to cross over now. And I want to thank them for all the info. I don't think it will open tomorrow. They'll have to check out the priest hole first."

Hayley held up a finger and Luna jumped off her lap and made for the hall. "Tom's coming."

Betty said, "I would have loved to have that ability to sense when John was on his way so I could jump up and look busy."

Hayley smiled. "I heard the car door slam, hun. But it's

uncanny — Luna always knows when he's due home. Perhaps he won't know you're here if I don't say anything."

Tom was never too pleased when they had company when he got home from work. Abigail could never understand why.

But this time Benjie gave it away. After smiling and holding his arms up to his daddy, he pointed to an empty space and started jabbering. The final straw had been when the little boy had said his first word. It wasn't dada, even mama. No, it was aba.

"They're here, aren't they?" he said with a sigh.

"They'll be off soon, hun. We were just filling in Lillian and Suzie. They weren't there. And you must admit, they were very handy today."

"Er, if you say so. Yes, thanks to them, I got to go into a spider-infested room and find a horrible corpse in a barrel. Please thank them for me."

"Ah, but now you've found the tunnel you'll be able to find Mrs Drayton."

Tom looked surprised and smiled. "So they don't know everything. We already know where Mrs Drayton is."

"Oh no, Tom, I was hoping that she would still be alive somewhere."

"Oh, she is, Hayley. Very much so. She turned up at The Three Crows wanting to know why her husband wasn't home."

Abigail said, "That's a bit fishy. She would say that if she'd killed him."

But Hayley said, "And Johnson believed her?"

"You know him, he doesn't believe anyone. Her story is that her mum was babysitting and the baby wouldn't stop crying, so she left about three or four. She rang for a taxi and went, so she's been at her mum's house. We never checked there. She left the car for Tyler because he had all the equipment. Could be true. And she seemed genuinely in shock. But murderers are often good actors. They've even fooled you at times."

"You're right, Tom. But poor woman, that must have been a hell of a shock for her. Could any of the others corroborate the time she left?"

"Damien heard a car go off about then, but he couldn't say if it was her or not. They'll check with her mother and the taxi driver tomorrow."

"So another suspect then, hun."

"I tell you what, I'll take Benjie to bed and leave you to talk." Tom turned and said, "Night to the rest of you. And thank you for your help today."

"Did he just thank us? Miracles do happen," said Abigail.

"Thanks, hun. I'll be up in a bit." To Abigail she answered, "He's always grateful. Sometimes anyway."

"Tell him you might need to pop out for five minutes," said Abigail.

"Now? If I must. Tom, I might need to pop out quick," Hayley shouted up the stairs.

"Where to?"

"I have no idea. I'll let you know when I get back."

Tom shook his head. At least life wasn't dull. "Come on, Luna. Us boys might as well go to bed and watch TV."

"So what have I got to do?" asked Hayley. "It's alright for you lot. You don't need to get your beauty sleep."

"You haven't got to do anything, and you're beautiful enough. But we do need a lift somewhere, then you can get off home. I think we ought to start visiting the guests to see who's the real deal and who could have cheated. And we should start with the celebrity at the Courtridge Hotel and Spa."

Chapter 8

ALL OF THE GHOSTS ENTERED THE GROUNDS OF THE hotel where they had investigated a murder and a few years ago, had been a castle. Once again Abigail was impressed by the giant lobby. The receptionist was busy with a guest, and so Lillian talked Suzie through checking on the computer to see what room Damien Shadow was in.

Lifts could be a bit tricky, they had found in the past, so they walked up the stairs to room eighty-nine. They would have liked to knock, but walked through the wall and just hoped he was dressed. Well, Betty wasn't worried either way, as she told Lillian, "He is a bit of a hunk. Not a patch on my John, of course."

The good-looking television star was sitting on the edge of his king-size bed. Terry couldn't help but laugh.

"I'm sorry, ladies. Smoke and mirrors, I think they call it."

"Yesss," said Abigail slowly. "Still handsome though, kind of."

"Yes, dear. Not quite the same as before. He reminds me of my grandad," said Betty.

"Was he handsome?"

"No, he put his teeth in a glass at night as well." Betty pointed to his bedside table where there were Damien's sparkling white teeth, a lustrous wig and a little tray containing two bright blue contact lenses. "Here's his credit card; it says his name is actually Wilbert Pidley. He's still a man's man though."

To spoil the illusion completely, the hotel's phone rang and they heard him say, "Hello, dear, yes, dear. You won't believe the day I've had. First …"

"Oh, don't mind me, Wilbert Pidley. I've been stuck here all day and you're in a luxury hotel. I wish I could have a day at the spa."

His wife ranted for a few minutes until her husband could get a word in and tell her that there had been a murder at the event. Then she shut up as she wanted to know all about it. But as Abigail walked towards him, he stopped.

"Sorry, Mavis, I've got to go," and he cut her off mid-sentence. He stretched out his hand and felt a cold column of air.

"Is there anybody there? Please make yourself known. Show yourself."

Abigail said, "So it shows he's not a total fake. Give the man what he wants, Suzie. Touch him."

"Which one? The one sitting on the bed or the one on the cupboard?" she giggled.

Suzie squeezed the medium's forearm and he jumped up. If he had had any hair, Abigail guessed it would have been standing on end.

"Thank you," he stuttered. "Do you mean me any harm?" Damien looked for his phone and then remembered he had given it to the police. "What is your name?"

"It's times like this I wish we could communicate," said Lillian.

"We could do it old school," said Terry. "Suzie, pick up that wine glass and put it on the bed."

Damien must have been braver than they thought, because he got the hint and got his ouija board out and put it on the coffee table. "What is your name?" He went to put his finger on the planchette but he didn't have to. It shook and moved on its own.

The spirit board spelt out 'SUZIE'. Then 'YOU KILLED TYLER'.

"No, of course not. I have no idea who did."

'DO NOT LIE TO ME'.

Damien had a horrible feeling that there was more than one ghost in the room, and even a demon. He knocked the board to the floor and ran to the bed and hid under the covers. They could hear him reciting the Lord's Prayer.

"After all these years you'd think he would be glad of a bit of proof," said Terry.

"I can't blame him," said Lillian. "I'd have been out of the door."

"At least we know he is clairvoyant. Not like Hayley, but he is. I have a feeling he'll never be able to match what happened tonight. Let's go," said Abigail. "I don't think he's a murderer."

Betty looked over at the parts of Damien that weren't under the covers. "Who said, 'Never meet your heroes,' Abigail?"

"I don't know, but they were right."

After five minutes, Damien had a feeling that Suzie and the other spirits had gone. The most fascinating thing that had ever happened, and he hadn't been able to film it. The police had his camera and his phone. Damien decided he'd come back to the Courtridge and bring a film crew. He knew the lot from the coaching inn would never believe him, but some might. Especially if he could just find out who Suzie was.

Chapter 9

TOM HAD TO BE AT WORK EARLY TO DRIVE JOHNSON TO Priory Lodge. He thought the constable would be more useful if someone had to go down a dark passage than his sergeant. It was away from the road in the middle of open, barren land and had a narrow drive leading up to it. It must have seemed very desolate and remote in the past. There were two gables and none of the ornate beams like The Three Crows. The tiny windows were made smaller by the ivy that had taken over most of the front façade.

"It looks more like a house in a horror film than a religious one," said Tom.

"Let's hope you don't have to go in the cellar or attic here then, lad."

The front door was opened before they got out of the car by a well-dressed lady in her fifties.

"I expect you're the police. We heard about the murder. Come in. I'm Stella Brooksby, the local doctor."

"DCI Tony Johnson and my PC from Gorebridge CID. Is your husband at home? We'd like to speak to you both."

"Come through. He's out the back doing the pruning."

Stella led them through the kitchen and out into a garden that looked a lot better than the front. Even though summer had nearly gone, there was still an abundance of flowers. Two concrete lions marked the edge of the terrace where they saw a man with some secateurs in hand.

"Major Brooksby? Lovely garden," said Tom.

"Thank you. We had it landscaped a few years ago. My wife likes the lions. I prefer the flowers and shrubs to be the focus."

"I like the wishing well," said Tom.

"That was already here," said Stella. "It's only ornamental now. But I believe it once supplied the priory with all the water they needed."

"When my green-fingered constable has finished talking about the garden, could we get back to the murder?"

The major said, "We don't know anything about that. But it's our local, so we often go in there. I suppose the last time was the Wednesday before last. And we know not to go when they have one of their paranormal weekends."

"That's why we've come here, sir. The pub is just behind that hedge, isn't it?" asked Tom. "We found a priest hole and we suspect there's a tunnel that comes from the old priory. There might be an easier access from here. Then we can get forensics to check it."

The major sighed. "Then you'll be as disappointed as us. I spent my childhood looking for it. My father bought the house in the sixties and was told about one, but we never found it. We had no end of building work done and the builders never saw one."

Stella added, "We had a huge basement conversion done and they never mentioned a blocked-up entrance."

"No secret rooms behind panelling or bookcases? What about the back of a wardrobe that leads somewhere?"

"We're not looking for Narnia, lad. Excuse him, Major."

"Actually, we have checked all the built-in wardrobes. Especially our two children when they were young. It's a perfectly good idea, Constable."

Johnson turned to go. He didn't want to hear anyone else praise him. Somehow it had got back to the Chief Constable that Tom had found the body in the cellar and the secret room.

"Well, thank you both for your help. Tom here will just have to go in from the other end. So listen out for any knocking if he gets through."

Dr Brooksby looked concerned. "Maybe it's collapsed over the years. Are you sure it's safe for him to go in there?"

"He'll be fine," said Johnson, with a wicked look at the young PC. "He's looking forward to it."

Chapter 10

SERGEANT DAVE MILLS WAS MORE THAN PLEASED that Tom had gone with the boss to see the Brooksbys and that he was to talk to the elderly lady in the shop. He parked in the pub's car park and walked up the street to the 'Village Stores'. It seemed a very poor idea of a village to him. One pub, one shop, no church, just a village hall. The terraced houses were shabby and small and lined either side of the road. There were a few bigger houses on the other side of the green, but Mills guessed there were probably only two hundred people at the most who lived there.

A small bell tinkled overhead as he went down the worn step. It was like going back in time. It reminded him of a corner shop he had gone into once on holiday in the Lake District. At first he couldn't see Miss Trippet. There was nearly as much for sale as in a supermarket. There were gardening tools, teapots, newspapers, books, groceries, even a post office in the far corner.

"Police, I can tell," said a shaky voice. Dave thought the small, white-haired lady to be in her late eighties.

"Sergeant Dave Mills. I've been told if I want to know about the history of Grimbles Cross to talk to you, Miss Trippet."

"It's true. But I know nothing about the death of that man. But I'm not surprised about it. Nor about the body in the barrel."

"Why's that?"

"Because this village is cursed, Sergeant. It was a mistake not to build a church here. It attracted the ungodly, you see. Thieves and vagabonds were drawn here in the past. I'm not saying they are now. There's some lovely people living here. But when the pub was built, that brought even more here. I say all about it in my book."

"You're an author?"

"I wrote a non-fiction book about the area, so fire away. What do you want to know?"

"We found a priest hole in the pub, next to the old fireplace. We think it drops down into a tunnel that went from the priory. Do you know anything about it?"

"How exciting. I knew there was one that went from the priory when the monks were forced to flee, but no one knew where it went to. Or where it started. I remember my granny telling me about it. It may still exist. Are you going to go through it?"

"Not me personally, I'm glad to say."

"Do let me know. Of course, this area is mainly chalk, so it would have been quite an easy task to dig out a tunnel, even back then. Which might also mean that's why it crumbled and disappeared. If it went to the priory it wouldn't have needed to be that long. A hundred feet as the crow flies, if you'll forgive my little joke. So who told you about the hole? I'd be surprised if it was Emma and Louise who run the pub. They paid a lot to take it over, but they don't seem interested in the history of it."

"No, they didn't know about a tunnel. I can't say officially, but if you're thinking of writing another book, it may well have been with the help of a ghost or two."

"Grimble is riddled with ghosts, Sergeant. There's a burial tor near here for one thing. And as I said, it was a very lawless area; hence the gallows. Before that, they were strung up from the oak tree. Without a trial sometimes. I called one chapter *Highwaymen and Harlots*. They talk about Murdering Megan, but my granny said it was Madam Megan. As you know, it's the oldest profession. She's one of the ghosts that are said to haunt The Three Crows. I've never seen any myself, but I've heard them. Horses' hooves on the cobblestones, and on a quiet night you can hear soldiers marching. I think they might be a Roman legion, but others have seen them and say they look like they're from the Civil War era. There was a battle further north."

"I remember learning about it at school. I think it was the Battle of Cadderly Bridge."

"That's right, Sergeant. The Roundheads and the Cavaliers. They say even Cromwell himself was there. Do you remember the year?"

"No, I don't. My history teacher would be very disappointed."

"1642. I write about it in my book. Old farmer Skirmet was forever finding bits and pieces when his horse was ploughing the fields. Mostly things of no value, like broken pots or coins. But he did find part of a gold belt buckle that he sold to a museum."

"Well, look at the Staffordshire Hoard. That was found by a farmer. He got over a million. Wonder no one has gone there with a metal detector."

"They have. They found a few coins and bits of weapons, but that's all."

"So tell me about Grimbles Priory."

"It was built for Benedictine monks. Parts of it date back to the fourteenth century, and there've been bits added on over the years. Then, in the sixteenth century, Henry VIII began his Dissolution of the Monasteries. A dreadful period. Since then it's been a school, a hospital, a convent, and it housed troops in both of the world wars. The Brooksbys bought it after that and made it into a house. Rather a depressing one, in my eyes. I think, with the history, it will never be a happy home."

"My inspector is up there now talking to the Major."

"He's married to our local doctor, Stella. She's a lovely lady. The Major is a typical military man; retired now. They've got a daughter at university and a younger son still at home. I have to watch him in here. Alcohol can go missing. I even caught him behind the counter with a packet of cigarettes. I let him off with a warning for his mother's sake. It would deeply upset Stella if she knew."

"Well, that's all very helpful, Miss Trippet. Is your book still available?"

"I just happen to have one here. That's ten pounds, please. Oh, and Sergeant, make sure you read about the legends of the crows. They were there last night and were still there this morning, so don't say you haven't been warned. This village is cursed, and don't you forget it."

Mills walked back towards the pub and looked up at the crows that were painted on the sign, which was creaking as it blew in the wind. She was right. It did feel like there was a curse over the village. Maybe by one of the monks, or even one of the poor souls that had lost their life dangling on the end of a rope. Dave couldn't wait to get this one solved and never have to come back to this depressing place again.

It got more depressing when he heard Johnson's voice shouting at Tom.

"You'll be fine. Come on, get your overalls and gloves on. Here, I've got a hard hat for you. See how I think of you?"

"That's not going to help if the whole roof collapses on me."

"Just make sure you go through gently. If it comes down we

could lose all the evidence. Keep your radio on. And I've even got you a big torch and a mask," said Johnson.

"Very thoughtful, sir," sighed Tom.

"Mills and I will be right behind you. Not right behind, obviously. But you'll be out the other end in no time."

"If I do come out."

"If not, you'll have to reverse. I've put Jane Nichols at Priory Lodge and she'll be there to open the door or whatever."

Tom put on his yellow hat and mask as Emma and Louise joined them and asked if they could film it on their phones.

"I suppose so," said Johnson. "Did the police photographer and forensics come earlier?"

"They did, and took away Tyler Drayton's equipment. They said they'll be back later, depending on what you find."

"Well, bye, Bennett. It's been nice knowing you. Joking, lad. Hat on and keep your radio on."

Bob had left an electric spotlight in there that lit up the entire secret room. The lead was long enough that Tom could lower it into the passage and light up a short way. He could see that he wouldn't have to go on his hands and knees, but walk bent over. He thought that people must have been a lot shorter in those days.

"It's definitely a tunnel, sir. About five feet high and three across. Here goes."

All was quiet, and Mills was starting to worry, so he said, "What can you see, Tom?"

"History. It's a funny feeling. There are little alcoves dug out in the walls every so often in the chalk. And you can see the candle wax still there. Makes it seem real. The air is getting a bit thin. I'll have to not talk for a while."

After three minutes of silence Johnson called out to Tom. He started panicking at the thought that something could happen to the young lad and he would get the blame. Health and safety and all that rubbish.

"I'm okay," Tom replied eventually. "I can see light in the distance. I think I'm nearly there."

"So there's no door?"

"No. The whole thing is just an opening. It could come out in the grounds. I'm nearly there. I can see brickwork now. I'm there. Just getting out. Woah, I nearly fell. God, that was close. You'll never guess where I am, sir."

"No, I won't. So tell me," snapped Johnson.

"I'm in the well, sir. That wishing well in Major Brooksby's garden."

So Mills and Johnson made for the old priory, and the Brooksbys followed them into the garden where WPC Jane Nichols was waiting by the well. They peered over the edge but couldn't see a thing. No hole or gap in the bricks, or the young constable. All they could see was blackness, possibly water, at the bottom twenty feet below.

"Bennett, where the devil are you?"

A yellow head appeared about nine feet down from the top, and Tom turned his head to look up at them.

"Here, sir."

"Well, bugg… sorry, Doctor. Well, I'm blowed. You can't see a thing from up here."

"With the bricks it's like an optical illusion," said Mills. "No wonder no one could find it."

The major said, "How wonderful. Puzzle solved at last."

"Can I get out now?"

"Not yet, lad. Did you see any bodies in there?"

"A couple of rats, dead, luckily. That was all."

Mills pulled the rope and wooden bucket towards him. "This must have been how the monks got up and down."

"It does look a bit lower than usual, but I wouldn't have noticed," said the major.

Mills pointed and said, "Look at that. If you look closely,

there are small footholds made of brick, so you'd never notice them. Obviously, it wouldn't have been this rope."

"My father replaced the rope and bucket that were there. They'd rotted away. It's just for show, really. We'd put a board across when the children were small. We didn't want them going head first, and took it off about ten years ago. The only time we come near it is when someone throws a coin down and makes a wish. That happens quite a lot. There must be quite a bit of cash down there. I did think about putting up a sign for a charity, but never got round to it. I'll have to tell the kids. They'll be thrilled to hear about it. Especially our son."

"Can I come up then, sir? My back's going."

Mills undid the rope. "I'll lower the bucket and you can grab the rope. It looks strong enough."

Tom got up safely and pointed to something snagged on a splinter on the wooden bucket. "A few fibres of cloth, sir."

"Don't touch it, we'll get Bob here. Looks like a bit off a red shirt or blouse." Wasn't the wife in red, thought Johnson. She could have come out here and then got a taxi.

"That's more a bright burgundy," said Tom.

"Thanks, Ralph Lauren."

Stella Brooksby frowned and squinted at the torn threads. "That looks a bit like my son's jacket. I'm sure it's not, but he wasn't in his bed yesterday morning. I assumed he must have left early." She looked down at the depth of the well into the stagnant water. "You don't think?"

"I'm sure he's fine," Mills said kindly. "We'll look for him. What's his name?"

"Sam, actually Samuel."

"And he's gone AWOL, has he, Major?" said Johnson pointedly.

"Not at all, and I don't like your tone. He's a teenager, so they often do their own thing. It was a Saturday night, and I should imagine one of his friends had a party and he stayed over."

"So what does your son do for a job? Could he be there?"

"He's still looking at his options after leaving school, Inspector."

"So he's doing nothing. I suppose you can if your family has money."

"It's not like that," said Samuel's mother. "He's a sensitive boy and he's had a few problems. And it doesn't help that his sister is a gifted scholar. But just lately he's sent off some job applications that he's waiting to hear back from."

"Have you tried his mobile?"

"Of course we have. I've been trying since yesterday morning. He may have been there before I went in at lunchtime. It's just unusual for him to be up before twelve on a Sunday. Or any day."

"Hmm. So you're telling me that you haven't seen your son since a man was brutally murdered near here. And now we have physical evidence that shows he had access to and from the scene. Hmm," said Johnson again.

Major Brooksby snapped, "What are you saying? Surely you don't think my boy has anything to do with the murder? That's ridiculous."

"Well, he is missing. Tom, secure the crime scene, lad. We'll need to search your son's room."

"Don't you need to have a warrant to do that?"

"If you want to wait, we can get one."

Stella disagreed. "No, please go ahead. I'm going to try his phone again. I know Samuel's a good boy, so I need to know he's safe. Come on, I'll show you his room."

Mills asked, "Is there any girlfriend we could talk to? Any good friends?"

"No girlfriend that he's told us about," said Stella.

"He's got a few local friends; Max and Calum are two of them," said the major with a sneer.

"Calum King?"

"Yes, do you know him?"

"You could say that."

"I'm not surprised the police have heard of him. If Sam ever got into mischief it was with Calum King. Not that that would include murder."

"Young Calum was at the Crows last night when the murder took place."

"Well, there you are then."

"Wasn't Samuel interested in this ghost stuff?" asked Mills.

"Not that I knew of. He preferred zombies. He was always killing them in his room late at night. Not that it means anything. He wouldn't have gone to that sort of thing."

"Ring Calum, he must know where Samuel is," said Stella.

"We will be talking to him, don't worry. It's all becoming a lot clearer," said the inspector, rubbing his hands together. This was going to be a lot easier than he thought. Two young lads meet up, get up to God knows what, and get caught by Tyler, so they kill him. No doubt high on drugs, he thought.

Mills and Johnson followed the parents into the house. It was as gloomy upstairs as it was downstairs. The Brooksbys showed them into a typically messy boy's bedroom and left them to it.

"So what exactly are we looking for, sir?"

"Start in the drawers. Drugs, I reckon, Dave. Met up with his mate, Calum, and things got out of hand. It must have been Sam; the tunnel goes from here. Gloves on, son."

"Laptop here. Smell that, sir," Mills said as he opened the desk drawer.

"Marijuana. Try and find something a bit stronger."

"There's this," said Mills as he opened the wardrobe. At the back was something that impressed his boss.

"We were looking for Narnia, but we found Nirvana. Look at all those lovely bottles," said Johnson.

"Lagers and quite a few bottles of Grimble Goblin beer. And vodka. I'm betting from the inn. But does this mean he came back here and stashed them and then went? Seems unlikely," admitted Mills.

"More than likely. Ask the mum if any of his clothes are missing. Then call the station; I want a full search done. The parents could be hiding something as well. It's means, motive and opportunity. I don't see a wallet, do you? I bet he's trying to leave the country. Let's get back and put out an APB. I'll give a news conference later. Go and get a recent photo of Samuel Brooksby for us to use. I'm going to call the Chief Constable and tell him I've solved another case."

Chapter 11

Tom rang Hayley as soon as he could. Not for an update, but because she was worried that Johnson was going to make him go in the tunnel. But once she knew that he had survived, she wanted to know everything. Then she joined the others in the library. As usual, they were sitting at the back. Tilly, the ginger ghost cat, was playing with Suzie on the floor.

"So the monks would climb down and go to the pub when they were in danger," said Terry.

"Or just hide in there. Tom said there were places for candles carved out in the chalk. He said there were no skeletons, so they must have made it out again. But this is the most interesting part. Do you remember the old lady that asked me to find her grandson?"

Abigail did. "Samuel, was it?"

"Apparently, Major Brooksby's son is called Samuel and not only is he missing, a bit of his jacket may have been found in the well. And one of his mates was Calum King, so they'll be checking on him. Samuel's about eighteen, and Mills said he's been caught shoplifting from the village shop before."

"I should think it's every teenager's dream to have a secret passageway to a pub full of free alcohol," said Abigail. "So did Samuel get caught by Drayton and kill him? Or did he see the murderer kill Drayton? He's either dead or on the run."

"Tom said that Johnson has already put out an arrest warrant for him. He's convinced he's got his man."

"He's not a man though really, is he? I think he's still a boy. I do hope he's on the run," said Betty. "How awful for the parents if he's dead. I really couldn't have gone on if one of my children had died."

"I know what you mean since I've been a mum. So it must have been his grandmother that scared me half to death. She knew something had happened. I'll look for her when I go to the pub tomorrow. I'm hoping Lady Caroline will meet me there for a chat. I might have to go and see Dr Brooksby at one point. I have a bad feeling about it."

"Has Tom said anything about the other suspects?" asked Terry.

"They're checking alibis and times still. The two young girls, Julia and Mia, were seen going into their room when they said, and Damien heard them talking. And they hadn't met Tyler, so they're more or less cleared."

"You mean they said they had never met him. I never believe anyone. Especially if they've got an alibi. One of them could have crept out and the other one talked to themselves," said Abigail. "Did Rachel's mum confirm the story about the baby being ill?"

"Yes and no. Rachel said she had a call to say the baby was poorly, but the mum said that Rachel had rung her to check on him. She got back just after half four. But Tyler could already have been dead by then."

"Did she know about the priest hole?"

"She denied it, but they checked and she was born and bred in Grimbles Cross, so maybe she did. Her family moved away when she was fifteen."

"She's a possible then. I think Hayley Moon should pay her a visit," suggested Betty. "I'm betting the dollar on my bottom that it's Luke King and nothing to do with Samuel. I wonder if his alibi is his son and Calum's is his. Why don't we go and see them to see how psychic they really are, and have a bit of a snoop? And the other ones."

"I'll get their addresses from Tom. What do we know about the two sisters, Terry?"

"Both single. Emma through choice. Louise told Johnson that she'd had a tough break-up with—er—Cameron, I think she said. They bought the pub about two or three years ago. After they served the drinks, they closed the bar and went to their room at the top of the pub and locked the door to keep the others out."

"Would one have heard the other one leave?"

"Probably. All the stairs are creaky. But they were adamant they didn't know about the priest hole. I mean, if they had, surely they would have told people and got more customers in. And ghost hunters."

"The police did a check and didn't find anything in their records. But we'll keep an open mind. Now, if you don't mind, I'm going home to see my poor husband. Johnson said he could get off early and clean up."

"Do you want us to come with you?" asked Abigail.

"I think he's suffered enough today, hun."

"Well, that's charming. I was only going to see if there was any more news. I'm not one to stay where I'm not wanted. What?" said Abigail, blinking quickly.

"There's a saying," said Betty, which made them all get to their feet. "Now what was it? About taking fish round to someone's house."

"I wouldn't like that, hun, thank you."

"Not even a red herring?" joked Abigail.

Betty waved her hands to get them to be quiet. "I'll have it in a minute."

"Just one?" said Abigail.

"Ye of little faith. See, I got that one right. I know, 'Guests, like fish, begin to smell after three days'."

"Well, that's not right, Betty," said Abigail. "It only takes me one day to wear out my welcome."

Tom would agree with that and was glad it was just his wife and son there when he got home. And Luna, of course. When Hayley had first brought the nearly dead kitten home, he hadn't wanted it. But now he loved that cat. As much as he loved Benjamin, not that he would admit that to anyone. It always wanted to sleep with him and was definitely his favourite human. Which didn't please Hayley, as she was the one that had to pander to Luna's every need.

Tom sat on the sofa and patted it for Hayley to sit down next to him. He had some sad news, that seemed even worse now that he was a father.

"What is it, Tom? I know it's bad news."

"We got a ladder and Bob checked the bottom of the well. There was about three feet of water and in there was a body."

Hayley knew right away. "It was Samuel Brooksby, wasn't it?"

Tom put his arm around her. "It was, love. How did you guess that?"

"It wasn't a guess. I had a feeling there was something wrong."

"The parents were heartbroken. I kept thinking of Benjie. His mum literally collapsed on the floor. Major Brooksby tried to keep it together, but even his training couldn't stop the grief coming out. They insisted on being there when he was lifted out as well. Once Dr Brooksby had seen him, she said she had to go and phone her daughter. Just as well. I think she was telling herself it was an accident. You could tell the Major didn't."

"And was it an accident? I'm hoping he fell and died quickly."

"It might have been quick, but it wasn't an accident."

"Not another murder? How do they know?"

"Dr Malik said he'd been strangled, probably from behind. They don't know by what. But it could have been a strap about an inch or so wide. She'll do the autopsy tomorrow."

"I'll have to tell his grandmother. She knew something had happened."

"I'll let Mills know. How do you know her?" Hayley just raised her eyebrows in answer. "Oh, I see. Perhaps I won't mention it then."

"I looked in the car mirror and she was sitting in the back seat staring at me. I hate it when they do that. She always felt she had to look after Sam and she was worried because she couldn't find him. Breaks my heart. It's worse when they're young."

"He would've been nineteen next month, that was all."

"I bet Johnson was shocked. He'd got him down as the killer, hadn't he?"

"Spitting feathers, big crow ones. He'd got the reporters and cameras all ready, but to give him his due, he didn't even blink. Just said it was all down to his department that they searched the well and found the body of poor, young Samuel Brooksby."

"You have to give him credit. But I suppose he wasn't going to eat crow, was he? Sorry, hun, I shouldn't joke. I've been with Abigail too much."

"If we didn't see humour in things, I don't think I could do this job. Without you, I wouldn't get out of bed after a day like today. I love you, Hayley Bennett. I'm even quite fond of Hayley Moon sometimes."

"I love you too; my husband and the policeman. Just one thing though, how did Samuel find out about the tunnel?"

"I was thinking about that on the way home. The major said

loads of people made a wish and threw a coin down the well. It looks like an old wishing well, if you know what I mean. Maybe at some point he needed the money for, say, cigarettes and climbed down. Then he saw the hole in the side. And Bob did say that there were only about ten coins down there that they bagged up, so I'm thinking he'd taken the rest. And there was Samuel's phone and torch with him."

"Do you know when the pub will be allowed to open? I'm going to meet Caroline for a drink and hopefully see Samuel's gran. I'm not looking forward to telling her. But I expect she already knows by now. She must have been to Priory Lodge since then."

"They can open tomorrow. There's no more evidence there. And you know what? I want you to let Abigail have free rein. She can do whatever she likes on this one. I want this murderer caught. Tell her she can stick her nose in as much as she wants."

"Oh, Tom, you must be upset. Come here, hun. You want to know how much I love you?"

"How much? It's been a while," he said cheekily.

Hayley took his hand. "Benjie's asleep, come on, I'll show you."

Luna got up too. Good idea, he felt like an early night himself. The cat next door had been in his garden and so he missed his third afternoon nap. What he didn't expect was for the bedroom door to be firmly shut in his face. What was going on? After getting no response after meowing, the disgruntled cat went downstairs. He looked at his scratching post and then at the armchair and got to work. They had to learn who was in charge.

Chapter 12

Hayley had arranged to meet Lady Caroline Hatton at The Three Crows at twelve-thirty. The agency had become friends with her when they investigated a case at Chiltern Hall. She knew all about the spirits and always wanted to help them when she could.

Hayley had got there ten minutes early in the hope of seeing Samuel's grandmother. But this time she was prepared when the woman appeared in her rear-view mirror.

"I'm glad you came. I've got some bad news for you. I know where Samuel is," said Hayley gently.

"So do I, my dear. He's sitting next to me."

Hayley spun round in her seat to see a fresh-faced youth in a burgundy jacket. Hayley looked for the sign of his death and noticed the redness around his throat and a graze down one side of his face. Whatever he had been strangled with was not there, so he must have died just after it was removed.

"Hi, Samuel. My name is Hayley. This is a surprise. I'm so sorry."

"Not as sorry as I am. My life is over."

"I know, hun. Do you know who it was?"

The Deadly Coaching Inn

"Who what was?" asked Samuel.

"Who killed you?"

Samuel looked at his gran. "I was killed? I thought I fell into the well."

"Tell us from the start. What were you doing at the well?"

"I must have been going to the pub to get some beers and tequila for a party. I think I must have fallen off the rope."

"Maybe. But they think you might have been strangled."

"Strangled? That can't be right."

"Try and think, Samuel. You were going to the pub along the passage. Then what?"

"Um, I was nearly there and I remembered there was one of those stupid ghost things on. Not so stupid though, is it? I was going to go back, but I saw someone open the door and drop some stuff down the hole. I had my torch on but I didn't see who it was, so I legged it."

"Do you think whoever it was saw you?"

"They couldn't have missed my torch. I wasn't waiting to find out, so I crawled out as quickly as I could. But somehow I don't remember getting to the other end. I thought it was my torch dying 'cos it went dark."

Hayley and Gran exchanged looks. That moment wasn't a torch dying, it was Samuel.

"I think that might have been when someone came up behind you, hun. But you have my absolute word that I'm going to find out who did it."

"Make sure you tell me first. Whoever it is will wish they were dead."

Hayley didn't like to tell him that he might not be able to get his revenge. But who knows? She had seen some strange things happen before.

"Where will you go?" asked Hayley.

"We'll be at the Lodge if you have any news," said the elderly lady. "My son needs me. How I wish I could hold him tight in his hour of need."

"I live in Becklesfield if you ever need me. But I'm sure me and my friends will be back here. And we won't give up till we find out who killed you and Mr Drayton. That's a promise."

Hayley watched as the pair walked away hand in hand, heads bowed. Knowing he was going back to a family he was no longer part of made her shed a tear. There was so much he was going to miss out on in life for no reason. Samuel had been a rebellious teenager, but he had plenty of time to turn that around and leave his mark on the world. She got out of the car and slammed the door. Sadness had become anger, and she walked with a new purpose into the bar.

It was beginning to get crowded. News of the murders had spread, and sightseers and journalists were there in groups. She recognised one reporter from the Chiltern Weekly and kept out of his way. As she looked over at the fireplace, her eyes locked with a scruffy-looking man with a red kerchief round his neck. She rather hoped he didn't know she could see him, but he did see the strange-looking lady with long black hair and beads, so he walked over.

"You must be Hayley. Morton Glasspool."

Hayley could only nod and carry on making her way through the tables to the bar. He would have to wait until she got a seat. She wasn't sure who was Emma and who was Louise, but she asked for one white wine and a water with lemon and took them to an empty table by the window. She was about to put her bag on the chair to save it for Caroline when Morton joined her.

"Yes, I'm Hayley. Hayley Moon when I'm working. I was sorry to hear what happened to you."

"Thank you for what you did. I'd still be in the cellar."

"I'm glad to help," she said behind her hand. "Which one is which behind the bar?"

"Emma has the lighter hair, and she's the oldest. Louise is

more of the barmaid and changes the barrels, and Emma does the other stuff. Times change, for sure. Who are you waiting for?"

"A friend of mine, Caroline."

"Well, I'll leave you to it, miss."

"Thank you. You're more thoughtful than some ghosts I could mention. I know one that doesn't like to miss a thing. Nosy but caring, as she calls it."

"That would be Abigail?"

"However did you guess," laughed Hayley, until she got a funny look from the next table.

Morton got to his feet. "I'm sorry about the young lad. We had seen him after hours a few times in the last weeks but didn't think much of it. We don't take much notice of what the living get up to. Poor boy. You find out who did it."

"We will. Abigail is tenacious, if nothing else. She's like a Jack Russell. Once she gets hold of something she doesn't let go."

"Shame she wasn't about when I was killed. I wish William Gillies had got what he deserved."

Hayley looked serious for a moment. "Don't worry about that. He got his punishment. I've seen the dark, swirling mist that takes them. You could move on, Morton, he won't be there."

"Good to know. But we'll see. I have to go to my burial first. See who's there."

"Let me know if you need any help, hun."

Morton moved away and sat on a small stool next to the hearth. Hayley sensed he spent many hours there in death. Watching, but not able to have any of the ale that he once loved. Hayley looked to the door and saw Caroline had arrived, and she waved as she went over.

"Lovely; a Chardonnay. You're not having one, Hayley?"

"I'm driving, hun."

"I brought the chauffeur. Well, he brought me, I suppose. I need a drink or two."

"Busy morning?"

"I had a meeting of the gymkhana committee. We got the photos back from the photographer. Do you remember him? We visited him when there was that murder at that wedding. He did a marvellous job."

"I do, Philip, isn't it?"

"That's right. We're going to make them into a calendar to sell for charity."

"Put me down for one," said Hayley.

"And while I think of it, he wanted your phone number, I hope you don't mind. He realised after he saw you that you were the psychic lady, and he took a photo in Ridgeway Wood the other day that he wants to talk with you about. He didn't say what."

"I don't mind at all. Well, there are quite a few ghosts in the woods, so I'm not surprised. I'll look forward to his call. But now for something much more important. How did the big date go?"

Caroline smiled and thought she was probably blushing like a schoolgirl. "Rather well, I think. That is, if you like being whisked away in a private helicopter, landing on a hotel roof in London and having dinner. Followed by tickets for the best show in town in a private box."

"I would have had worse dates. So I was right then," Hayley said proudly. It was nice to remember that she did get to predict the nice things in life sometimes, not just death. Not long ago, she had told the lonely Lady Caroline that she would meet a man with the initials JC. And soon after that, they were both introduced to Jasper Cravensby, the CEO of Cravensby Enterprises. The fact that he was one of the richest men in England Hayley had not foreseen.

"I'll never doubt you again, Hayley. Not that I ever did."

"So, I know he's got money, good looks and a helicopter, but is he a gentleman? Sometimes when they have it all, they think they're a cut above. And usually they are, but you're aristocracy, so that trumps all that."

"Not everyone is impressed by a title these days. But Jasper is so nice as well. You wouldn't know how rich he was to hear him talk. I think it's because he's a self-made man. He didn't grow up with much and started doing up old houses that no one else wanted. By himself to start with. Then he bought bigger houses. Sometimes from people like me, to pay for taxes and death duties. He'd turn those into golf courses and hotels. Remember Courtridge?"

"I'll never forget it after the murder there, hun."

"He bought the castle ruins, rebuilt it, and sold it to the American lady and made a fortune."

"That's amazing. I didn't know it was him. So what happened after the show?"

"As I said, he was the perfect gentleman and dropped me off in the Hall grounds with just a kiss. Shame."

"You do like him, I can tell."

"Who wouldn't? I'm seeing him next week for another date. He didn't say where."

"In his jet to Paris, probably," said Hayley.

"I do hope not. I prefer to travel on terra firma."

"At least it'll be a fancy car."

"I have no idea, I'll let you know. Are you eating here?" asked Caroline as she picked up a menu.

"I don't think I'll have time. Janine from the library is babysitting for me. So I'd better not take too many liberties."

"I'll look after him one of these days. I love the little man."

"I may hold you to that."

"Not that I know what to do with a child, but I'm sure Mrs Bittens will. She used to be a nanny. I can be fun Auntie Caroline with the big house."

"And married to Uncle Jasper with a helicopter and a fast car."

"Really? I've only been on one date."

"We shall see. Not that I'm saying you will. It's a bit early, even for me. And a lot can happen in life. As Tyler Drayton and Samuel Brooksby have found out."

"I've met Major Brooksby. The poor man has lost his only son. Although I should imagine he would have been a very strict disciplinarian. He doesn't suffer fools gladly, and I'm guessing neither misbehaviour in his children. I'm so pleased they found Samuel's body. They might never have thought of looking there if it wasn't for you knowing about the passage."

"And that was due to the ghosts here."

"Are there any here now?" she said excitedly. A couple of years ago, she would have been terrified.

"Morton Glasspool is. He's the one that was found in a barrel in the cellar by Tom."

"I'm not even going to ask," laughed Caroline. "So, talking of ghosts, where are your gang?"

"Abigail and the others are going to visit all the ghost hunters to see how good they are. The famous Damien Shadow seemed to be the real McCoy. He knew they were in his room but was terrified. Yet he claims to see them all the time. I suppose sensing and actually knowing for sure are two different things," said Hayley.

"I think if Abigail had suddenly appeared in front of me, I wouldn't have been so calm. Having you to introduce us was far more civilised."

"That's very true. After I've left here, I'm going to see the cameraman, Scott Clarkson. I've arranged to meet him in the Frimble Tea Room. I reckon he'll know what they get up to. And I'm hoping to have a word with the owners here. They're Emma and Louise Lockhart over there, serving behind the bar."

"A married couple?"

"I never thought of that. No, I'm sure someone said they're sisters. Well, that's what I've been told. I'm sure that Tom said neither of them had been married. But Louise had been engaged. But I'm not sure. It's a job to talk to them while they're so busy. I thought it would be empty."

Luckily for Hayley, and she had to admit that luck did often favour her, she saw Emma walking around collecting the glasses off the tables. She just had to think of something to strike up a conversation.

"Hi, Emma? I'm Tom's wife, Hayley. I believe he's been up your passage."

They all started to laugh. "I wouldn't say that, but I know what you mean. Although he is lovely, isn't he? A lot nicer than that Inspector."

"I'm very lucky. This is Lady Hatton. I don't know if you've met before."

"No. Pleased to meet you. I've heard of you, of course."

Caroline answered, "It doesn't look like the murder has been bad for business."

"No. I can't think why I didn't think of murdering one of the guests before," she joked. "The last few months have been very slow. We had to get rid of the full-time barman and the cleaner. It's been hard to cover for them. If it carries on like this, Sylvie and Clint can come back again."

Hayley tried to remember the names in case one of them, especially Clint, did not take kindly to being fired.

"I expect you do enough hours as it is," said Hayley.

"We never stop. And cleaning in a place like this is a nightmare. The old walls make so much dust, and look at all the wood that has to be polished."

"And brass, I should have thought," said Caroline. "I know from experience it can be a huge task." She didn't like to say that her experience was watching the staff do it.

"Has Tom said if they're near to arresting anyone yet?"

"They're still checking alibis and looking into who had a problem with Mr Drayton. Same with Samuel Brooksby."

"Fancy him knowing about the tunnel," said Emma.

"They think he might have known about it for a while and may have been coming in and out. Had you noticed anything going missing?"

"Lou keeps stock of the alcohol side of things. Looking back, she did say one of the spirit bottles had gone again. But you can't watch the bar all the time. Even more now that Clint isn't here. She has to go and change the barrels in the cellar, and you have to trust that the punters keep to that side of the bar."

Lady Caroline shivered and said, "I bet her blood ran cold when they found a body in a barrel. When you think of all the times she'd been down there on her own."

"It did mine. Louise is tougher than me, although she's younger. I'm a coward. Now Sylvie has gone I have to clean the rooms as well, and I've always hated going into Room six. I don't know if I can now. I can still picture that man on the bed."

"It's going to be a crime scene for a while, I expect," said Hayley.

"I know. But you know what? We've had so many calls and emails asking for that room. People are very strange."

"They are, Emma. They'll probably pay a fortune to see the priest hole as well. You've got a goldmine."

Emma picked up a glass and said, "If it goes quiet I'll just bump off another guest. Better go, Louise is giving me daggers."

"Nice lady," said Caroline. "I take it she was joking about bumping off the guests."

"If not she'll be a guest of His Majesty. I always thought it would be nice to run a pub till I spoke to the landlady at the Greyhound, and she said they never get any time off. And that's seven days a week, and when they close they have to clean up. Do you want another drink? It'll give me a chance to talk to Louise."

"If it helps the case, I'm sure I can manage another one, please."

Customers were two deep at the bar but Hayley eventually caught Louise's eye.

"Chardonnay and a sparkling water with lemon, please."

Emma came over. "Lou, this is that nice constable's wife."

She answered but carried on working. "Any news?"

"No, not yet. They think it might be one of the ghost hunters. Apparently Mr Drayton was calling one of them a cheat."

"We heard him say that, didn't we, Ems? So knowing that lot, it could be anyone. But I have faith that whoever did it will get punished," and Louise went off to serve the next customer.

Hayley picked up the drinks and thought she knew Louise was rushed off her feet, but she did not like that woman at all.

Chapter 13

ABIGAIL, TERRY, BETTY AND SUZIE WERE LOOKING forward to doing another assessment on one of the so-called clairvoyants. Abigail was surprised that Tom had agreed to the ghosts having the addresses of the suspects. Perhaps he was starting to mellow.

They arrived at Peter Peacock's home first. He lived in a block of flats on the outskirts of Gorebridge. When they entered his flat on the seventh floor, he was playing a video game, and it looked like he lived on his own. They decided against Suzie touching him this time. They needed to know if he was the empath that he told everyone he was. Hayley had found one of his videos online and he said he could feel the suffering of one of the ghosts at the old Chadly Courthouse. The spirit was distressed and terrified because he was in the condemned cell and was going to be hanged the next day. So it would have been an obvious guess.

"I know I can get annoyed with you, Abigail, but is that enough for him to feel my pain?"

"The trouble is I make you far too happy these days, Terry. How about if I sit next to him?"

Peter suddenly stopped what he was doing, but he got up and grabbed a can of beer.

"This is hopeless. He hasn't got a clue. All we're doing is wasting time," said Abigail. "I get so frustrated sometimes. If I was alive I could just…"

Peter turned his phone's camera on. "Guys, I'm sitting here and I can feel something next to me." He panned around the room. "Did you see that orb? I'm sensing a lost spirit. And anger. I think it's a woman. An unpleasant old woman."

"Old? See, I told you he wasn't any good," snapped Abigail.

"I think he's very good," laughed Terry.

"I'm only in my thirties."

"Thirty-nine, dear."

"Thank you, Betty."

"I think her name starts with the letter G. No, A. I'm getting Agatha."

"Well, I am like Miss Marple," said Abigail.

"Please show yourself. Or move something."

That was too much of a challenge for Abigail. "Serve him right for calling me old. Go on, Suzie."

She moved a cushion to the edge of the sofa and pushed it on the floor.

Unlike Damien Shadow, he gasped but also laughed. "Oh, my God, guys, did you see that? What is your name? Do you mean me any harm?"

"I do," said Abigail. "Old? I'll give him old. He's obviously a fraud. What are you two laughing at? Actually, let's go. He'll be more annoyed by that."

"So we don't think Tyler was referring to him then," said Betty.

"I do. He's at the top of my list now," replied Abigail.

But Peter Peacock didn't mind at all. He downloaded the video and had three thousand likes in the first hour.

The next paranormal investigator, as he called himself, was

Grant Mayfair. He lived in a shared house with three other young men. When the dead investigators arrived, he was in his bedroom sitting at his desk, still wearing his GPS T-shirt. He was watching all the footage he got from his night at The Three Crows, ready for his podcast. The police had reviewed it and returned it an hour ago.

Grant was replaying parts of it again and again.

He had an Electronic Voice Phenomena recorder that picked up various words that he was trying to make sense of: 'Walk - Coin - Roman - Fifty - Battle - Bridge - Follow'.

"See," said Abigail. "Just a load of random words." Not knowing it fit perfectly with all that Miss Trippet had told Dave Mills.

Suzie was scared when he played his footage as he went into the dark attic. They saw him filming the piles of boxes and tea chests, and a close-up of what he thought was an apparition but turned out to be his reflection in an old mirror. His hand jerked when he heard a crash from the other side of the dark attic and he swore.

Grant had said, "Did you hear that? I think it's a poltergeist. There's no one else in here with me. That noise came from behind that chest of drawers. And the temperature has dropped. And the EMF meter is going crazy."

Grant showed a close-up of his handheld gadget which was on red. He crept carefully forward.

"Is that you, Murdering Megan? How many people did you kill?" But Megan didn't answer so he paused the filming.

"That was a bit eerie," said Abigail.

Grant sat back and laughed. He said out loud, "No one will ever know I made that crash when I caught my foot on the lead of an old lamp."

"They will now," said Terry. "He could well be the cheater that Tyler was talking about. And we've been here ten minutes and he hasn't a clue."

Abigail told him, "But he hasn't got his thingy machine out or his laser whatsit. Or his cat's balls."

"He should see a doctor for that," said Terry as Suzie looked puzzled.

"Did he say he was psychic though?" said Betty.

"I don't think he did. He's got so much equipment, I think he's just interested in the supernatural. He's got books over there about UFOs as well. I didn't realise how popular ghost walks and tours were until Hayley showed us all the stuff on the computer. Think of the fun we could have if they came to Becklesfield Library one night," said Abigail.

"I don't think I'd like that," said Suzie. "I find it a bit scary. People walking about in the dark and making me jump."

"You'd be the one making them jump."

"I still wouldn't like it. Especially if they started saying there was a demon there."

Terry added, "And they might do a proper exorcism. I saw one of those performed once. It was a proper priest and everything. It was in an old house where some dead friends I knew were trying to get rid of the new tenants. They still thought it was their house. Anyway, this priest came and they disappeared quicker than a hat in a hurricane."

"I take it back then. No ghost hunters in the library. Apart from our Hayley. We'll pass on when we're ready."

Grant felt a slight breeze pass his left shoulder and shuddered. Could it be? Nah. He went back to looking at the footage. He fast-forwarded till he got to the old courtyard. He had to rewind a few times to be sure, but there was a shape that looked to be made out of white smoke. Grant zoomed in as much as he could. It looked like a child, possibly about twelve years old. A boy, probably. No, it was just a trick of the light. What a shame there were no ghosts about when you needed one, he thought as a group of them left him to ponder.

As Abigail and the others made their way to the King's house, Hayley was sitting with Scott Clarkson having a cup of tea and a slice of carrot cake. Hayley had told him in an email that she was a psychic medium who might need the help of a crew at some point.

"I looked you up. You're quite famous around here."

"I try not to be," said Hayley. "It's not the sort of thing you like others to know. It's a bit like when you're a hairdresser. Everyone you meet asks you to do their hair. With me, it's, 'Can you do me a reading? Or am I going to meet the man of my dreams tonight?'"

"I can imagine. So are you going to start a paranormal channel?"

"I might do. I heard you work a lot with Damien Shadow. That must be wonderful. Now he is famous."

"Not anymore. They want young and good-looking faces now. That's why he's doing these little events. He doesn't get paid, only his expenses. And he was a bit of an Ebenezer, if you know what I mean. So I don't get paid either. I got a night in a small pub room, that was it. There was a murder on Saturday at the last one. Did you know?"

"I did. It was someone called Drayton, wasn't it?"

"Yeah. So now Damien thinks he's going to get to the top again. He's already got a few interviews lined up. He's going on about a ghost called Suzie that visited him in his hotel room, so he's trying to find out what her connection is to the murders. It might turn out to be the best thing that's happened to him for a long time."

"You don't mean…?"

"I know he and Drayton couldn't stand each other. And the last I saw of Damien, he said he was going to bed."

"So he had a motive."

"Jealousy as well. I don't know if you've seen one of Tyler's shows, but they were good. He's got charisma and all the equipment. And the viewers loved him. He did one in an old house in Derbyshire that went viral. A shadow person appeared and disappeared out of the window. And a rocking chair moved on its own. I couldn't see any signs he'd done it. And of course, there's all the trouble he had with his poor wife."

Hayley was starting to enjoy herself. "Really? What was that?"

Scott leant back. "Hmm. I know exactly who you are, Hayley Bennett, or Moon. You are an investigator, but not into ghosts. Word gets around in these circles. Even people like Damien Shadow know they're no match for you."

"So you won't help me?"

"Not for free, no," said Scott.

Hayley got out her purse. "I think I might have thirty pounds. Or I could get some out. I'll gladly pay for our tea."

"I don't want money, Hayley. I want something worth far more."

Hayley was beginning to worry what she had got into. "Okay, what is it you want?"

"A reading."

"Oh, that I can do. Not now though. I have to be able to concentrate and see what I can channel."

"Okay, I can wait," said Scott.

Hayley felt a feeling of heaviness come over her. "But you can't wait too long, can you?"

"You know?"

Hayley felt her chest, where she pictured a black shadow. "I'm sorry, I do. How long have you got?"

"Maybe six months, if I'm lucky."

"I know already that you're loved on both sides. A man—actually, a boy—will be waiting for you. John, no, Jonathon."

"My best friend died in an accident about ten years ago.

Wow, I feel better already. I guess the rumours about you are true, Hayley."

"I can't do a proper reading here, Scott. I'll visit you when my head is clearer, I promise."

"Okay, what do you want to know?"

Chapter 14

THE LAST HOUSE THE SPIRITS HAD TO CHECK WAS THE one where Calum King lived with his parents. It was a semi-detached house not far from Becklesfield.

Calum was sprawled on the sofa with the television blaring and was looking at his phone. His mother was trying to tidy up around him.

"I thought you were going to look for a job. I'm sick and tired of you lazing about all day. We keep telling you, either you go to college or you get a job."

"I'm trying to get hold of Sam. I don't believe he's dead. He can't be. And I keep telling you, I don't know what I want to do yet. There's a lot to think about. It's my life."

Betty tutted and said, "If I was his mum, I'd throw him out of the nest. He's just swinging the leg."

Terry told her, "It's swinging the lead, Betty."

"Are you sure? I've been saying leg all my life and no one's said anything. You swing a leg, not lead, dear."

"It's one of those ship sayings. There's loads of them for some reason. Like 'loose cannon, cut of your jib, learn the ropes, batten down the hatches'."

"That one comes from chickens, I think, dear. Oh, and 'three sheeps to the wind'. I used to say that to my John when he'd had a few. Why you would have sheep on a ship, I have no idea."

Abigail said, "Could you two get back on dry land, please. Let's see if we can find his dad."

Luke King was on his laptop upstairs and was writing the newsletter for his website fans. He too had checked his investigation material and was rather pleased. He played the bit where he walked slowly down the creaky stairs and jumped as he said that someone had passed him who was going up. His whole arm had gone freezing cold, he said. Abigail, Betty and Suzie jumped as he filmed in the kitchen when a metallic sound of something dropping on the floor was recorded.

Luke put on the camera that had been recording while he was asleep in Room four. Nothing happened for about an hour and then they all heard the sound of running water. Luke played it three times.

"Could have been a toilet flushing and then filling up," said Suzie.

"It wasn't Luke, 'cos he's still in bed. We'll have to ask Tom if anyone else heard it. Could have been Room six, then we'll know Tyler was alive then. If it was after his wife left, that would make her innocent," said Abigail.

"Does this mean Luke's innocent? The time on that is four-twenty," said Suzie.

"Look at all his equipment. He could easily have stopped the tape for ten minutes. He's got more reason than anyone to cheat to make something happen. This is his livelihood. And he has no idea we're here."

Terry didn't agree. "But he never said he was psychic, just interested in the paranormal. He's a proper investigator. I would have loved to have done that. So what now?"

But there seemed to be something going on outside. Two cars had arrived and Suzie told them that she could see Sergeant

Mills. Luke King ran down the stairs two at a time. His wife was arguing with two uniformed officers who said they needed to search Calum's room.

Calum himself was being pulled to the back of one of the cars. So Abigail made a quick decision. She dragged Terry towards the same car and told Betty and Suzie to go back to Becklesfield and tell Lillian and Hayley that there had been an arrest for the murders of Tyler Drayton and Samuel Brooksby.

Chapter 15

"Calum King, you're not being charged yet, but..."

"So what am I here for? I haven't done anything."

DCI Johnson looked down at his notes. "Mrs Brooksby has told us that her son, Samuel, had a friend called Calum. Something you didn't mention when we asked everyone connected to the pub death after we found his body yesterday."

"I knew him a bit; we're the same age."

"How did you know him? He went to private school and I'm guessing you didn't."

"Can't remember now. At a friend's party, I think. Then I'd see him around here and there."

"Did he share your interest in the supernatural?"

"No. I only do it for Dad. Get him off my back about going to college. I'll go when I'm ready. Or just get a job."

"Or take up robbery, perhaps," said Johnson.

"Just because we're not as rich as the Brooksbys doesn't make me a thief."

"I can't imagine they'd be very happy about him being friends with you. Did they think you were leading him astray?"

"You're joking. He didn't need any help with that. The other way round, more like."

"We think there was a falling out of thieves in that tunnel and you strangled him."

"Rubbish. I didn't even know there was a tunnel. I would have told Dad if I knew."

"Hmm. See, that's where it gets a bit odd. Because we found your fingerprints in there. By the well and inside the panel at the other end. How can you explain that?"

Calum squirmed in his seat. "Okay, I knew about the tunnel. Sam told me about it after he'd found it. He'd been down the well trying to get some money that was in there and he saw the passage. For drugs, knowing him. His parents might say he's a saint, but he wasn't and they knew it. The Major had no time for him. Where was he when Sam was killed? He might have been waiting for him to come out. Maybe Sam had gone in the pub that night and he caught him with the drink. Wouldn't have done the Major's reputation any good. We went into the pub a couple of times at night and we helped ourselves to beer and that. But I bet he'd been other times."

"More likely that your mate turns up the night of the murder and nearly drops you right in it. So did he see you kill Drayton or did he catch you getting rid of the evidence? He wouldn't think much of it at the time, but he would the next day. Or did Drayton find you and him stealing from the bar? Maybe he was trying to blackmail Samuel. He's from a rich family. So one of you followed him upstairs with the toasting fork and killed him."

"I wouldn't kill anyone."

"My sergeant and I think you did. And maybe Samuel Brooksby didn't want to spend his life in jail to protect you, so you killed him before he could tell anyone."

"I didn't even see Sam that night. You check my phone, there's no messages from him to say he was going to be there."

"We checked, but you might have deleted them. And we can't check his. It's still full of water from being in the well, next to where we found his body. But our tech boys are working on it."

Mills spoke for the first time. "I'm wondering if it was you making stuff up that Tyler was talking about. Out of all the others, you're the only one that doesn't take ghostbusting seriously. Daddy wouldn't be too pleased. There's him thinking he's the new Van Helsing and you've been making it up as you go along. I reckon you've been kicking the cat's balls or pushing the glass."

"I'd never do that," but Calum's look said otherwise. "I think Tyler was threatening Damien Shadow. He's got more to lose than anyone."

"You mean Wilbert Pidley," Johnson told him. "We're still checking on him. But there's no proof he was ever in the Kings Arms in Amersford. Whereas you were on various occasions. Means, motive and opportunity, I would say, Mills. And what I don't think you're getting is that someone brutally killed Tyler and put his belongings in the hidden room. And you, by your own admission, are the only one there that night that knew it existed."

"I want my dad," said Calum with a break in his voice.

"I think you'd be better with a lawyer, son. Charge him, Sergeant."

Abigail stood up from the edge of the table and said to Terry, "Right, we need a meeting of The Deadly Detective Agency, fast."

Chapter 16

Abigail was very quiet on the number eight bus back to Becklesfield. She had a feeling she had about half the information she needed. Hopefully, Hayley would provide the rest. She herself was back from her meeting with Lady Caroline and Scott Clarkson, and was shocked, but not surprised, that Johnson had arrested Calum. She told them about Scott's sad news and how helpful he had been.

"He put a new slant on a few things. Scott said Rachel put up with a lot from her husband. He had a lot of female attention because of his show and podcast. One of Drayton's vigils had gone viral and was even shown as a clip on a few of the mainstream TV shows. He was actually on a couple of them talking about what happened. I wouldn't say they were groupies, but that kind of thing. Rachel turned a blind eye to most of it. But she was really unhappy that night, Scott told me."

"Because he'd been drinking?" said Betty.

"Yes, but not just that. Scott said she was annoyed because of who turned up."

"Ah, that makes sense," said Abigail. "The two young girls."

"Exactly. In particular Mia, Scott said. Rachel had seen her with him when he was supposed to be somewhere else. But Tyler denied it. No wonder Rachel left early. But she could have killed him first. Or did he tell Mia he wasn't interested anymore? No one has even looked at her. Her friend could be covering for her. So Scott has given us two more suspects. And I don't like to think it, but he seemed to have a genuine affection for Rachel. Could Scott have killed Tyler for Rachel because he knew even if he got caught, he wouldn't face much jail time?"

"But he wouldn't have known about the tunnel, would he?" said Terry.

"I've had a thought," said Betty. "What if Scott was getting rid of the camera and he saw Samuel coming out of the priest hole? So he chased him and left the camera there."

Lillian said, "But we know that Samuel never went into the pub. So Scott wouldn't know about it. And Calum is telling the truth as well."

"We actually heard Grant Mayfair admit that one loud bang was made by him and a lamp," said Suzie. "It could be him."

"All of them apart from Damien, Scott and the two girls were on that floor. Any of them could have crept down and got the fork and killed him after his wife left. Everyone said they heard creaking. I think Luke was the only one that heard running water. But he only heard that afterwards because he was asleep," said Terry.

"So he made out. I'll have to get Tom to ask them if they used the bathroom. If not, it could give a proper time of death. At the moment it's between four and six."

"I've got it," said Betty. "What's to stop Luke King from putting a pillow or his bag under the covers and then starting to record? My Jean did that once. I told her she couldn't go to a party and she did. Climbed out the window."

"I bet she was in trouble when she got home, hun."

"I didn't say a word, Hayley. I just locked the window and she had to sleep in the old garden shed from one in the morning. She never did it again. She'd already left and I didn't know where the party was, so I couldn't do anything. And who wants a big row in the middle of the night? I still laugh now when I think of Jean coming in the back door all covered with cobwebs and dirt. I should have grounded her for a month but that would have punished me more than her. She was a teenager."

"It's sad I'll never be a teenager," said Suzie.

"If it's any consolation, you won't be an old woman like me either, dear."

"I never think of you as old, Betty."

"What's that saying about getting old? With every year, I'm getting wider. Or is it wiser?"

"Definitely wiser!" said Abigail. "You've given me a very important clue."

"So I was right? Luke King did just pretend to be under the covers?"

"No, that was stupid. Let me think for a moment."

Betty whispered, "It must be the comment about teenagers then. So it must be Calum."

"Or those two young girls, hun."

"Mia, yes, that could be it." Abigail leaned back in the wicker chair in the conservatory and said to herself, "It could be that. But would that work?" She began moving her hands as if she were moving chess pieces.

The others knew not to talk at these times, but they always had a little giggle. That was everyone apart from Benjie. He chose that moment to throw his train and decide he was really, really starving.

"Good job he's cute," said Terry quietly. "If that was one of us she'd…"

"I heard that, Terry. Anyone would think I'm a right tyrant. You know me, others not self. What?" Abigail said. "Anyway, be quiet. Please."

"Will you be long, hun? He's only going to get louder."

Still with her eyes shut, Abigail held up a finger. "One second. Got it." She sat forward and said, "Now I know everything. As Betty would say, I've got all my crows in a row."

"Is it Calum, dear? Or Luke? Was I correct?"

"Nope. Sorry, Betty, I'm not going to tell you. We haven't got the time."

"Benjie can wait ten minutes, hun. I'll give him a biscuit. You carry on."

"I don't mean that, Hayl. We haven't got time because there could be another murder."

"Who?" they all wanted to know. Even Benjamin and Luna looked at Abigail expectantly.

"There are a few things I need to check first in case I make an utter fool of myself. Can you get Nanny Bennett to babysit?"

"To save a life, I can. Where are we going?"

"First, get hold of Tom and tell him to meet us there. Not Mills or Johnson yet. But we might need Tom."

"He finishes work in a bit. But where are we going, hun?"

"Grimbles Cross."

Chapter 17

Tom was already sitting outside The Three Crows when Hayley drove up. It looked like she was on her own, but Tom had no doubt that Abigail and the others were in there with her.

"What's all this about?" Tom asked as she got out.

"Our brilliant detective, Abigail, has it all figured out. And Johnson will have to release Calum."

"That's good news. But who's in danger?"

"She's telling me that she has to check something first. Let's go in and get a table, hun."

What they weren't expecting was to see DCI Johnson sitting on a stool at the bar and talking to the landladies.

"That's annoying. I'll get the drinks, you get a table," Tom said.

Hayley was a bit embarrassed that she had to choose the biggest table for the two of them, because the few customers that were there did not see all the ghosts from Becklesfield, as well as Friar Oswyn, Morton and Megan, join her.

"What the hell are you doing here, Bennett? As if I don't see enough of you at work."

"We managed to get a babysitter, so I thought I'd meet Hayley here for a meal."

"Well, keep away from me. I'm off duty," Johnson said as he winked at Emma.

"I've no problem with that at all," Tom answered as he took the drinks and sat down, after checking that no one else was sitting there. It was then that he saw the ghost hunters Peter Peacock and the bearded Grant sitting at a table together.

"What's going on then, Hayley?" he asked.

Hayley told him what Abigail wanted him to do first.

"I'll do it outside in case Johnson comes over." Tom got his phone out of his pocket and walked out.

Abigail got up as well. "Come on, Suzie, I need you to do something with me. No, just me and Suzie. I don't want to look stupid if I'm wrong."

They returned to the bar at the same time that Tom did. He took a sip of his shandy and nodded to Hayley.

Terry said, "Tom's never been at one of Abigail's denouements, has he?"

"What's that?" said Morton.

"It's when Abigail tells us who the killer is. Eventually. Usually in the style of Poirot and his little grey cells," which meant nothing to Morton either.

Abigail gave him a look and got to her feet. "As long as you don't say little grey hairs."

She felt she really should be in front of the fireplace, but she put her hands behind her back anyway and started.

"Okay, mes amis, it all started a few years ago. Tyler…"

"What's happening?" said Tom.

"She's just starting. It's not going to be quick, hun. I'll tell you as we go along."

"As we know, Tyler Drayton wasn't a very nice person. He liked to wind people up and Scott told us that he was unfaithful to his wife. And the more he drank that night, the nearer he got to being murdered. In the bar, before they split up, he accused someone of cheating. And it hit home. I'm guessing that all of the ghost hunters, if not cheated, exaggerated a bit or moved something for effect. Maybe his eyes lingered for an extra second as he looked around.

"And then he mentioned when and where this had happened. A few years ago, in a four-star hotel in Amersford. That person knew for sure then.

"Maybe that investigation had been a life-changing event for them. For instance, Damien Shadow's reputation would cost him everything. We know he's the real deal, but if one thing got out, everything else would be doubted. Same with all of them."

"It must have been Calum," said Betty. "He's the only one who knew about the tunnel. Samuel must have seen him."

"You're half right. Samuel did see someone getting rid of the evidence, but it wasn't Calum. Samuel had no idea who it was as he didn't actually see them, but the murderer couldn't take the risk. Samuel just didn't want to be found in the tunnel, so he made a hasty retreat. I bet he didn't know anyone was after him until he felt something go round his throat just before the end and he was pushed headfirst down the well.

"There were four clues that finally led me to the truth, helped by an observation from the brilliant Betty. The first one was the lever on the fireplace. Second was a belt. Third was the running water. And the fourth was when I heard about his relationship with Mia.

"But let's go back to what Tyler said. 'One of you cheated.' Now, what if it had nothing to do with the paranormal? What if it was what cheating usually means? Cheating at cards, or more likely, cheating on your husband or wife?"

"Luke's married. We saw his wife today," said Suzie.

"And Damien," said Betty.

Abigail said, "I think it was someone else. Hayley found out that Scott had a thing for Rachel; he could have been talking about his own wife and Scott cheating. Perhaps to shame them in front of everyone. Especially after she'd had a go at him for liking young girls. Maybe Tyler saw chemistry between them and remembered Scott had been at that pub in Amersford when Rachel had acted guilty. Emma told Johnson to ask Luke if he wanted to know about Rachel because they had been to a lot of the same events together. And I'm guessing that hotel. But I don't think Tyler would want to admit that about his wife and Scott in front of everyone. He was all about how he looked, so he would have been too ashamed. So I think we can discount them. But Scott and Rachel could have thought he was talking about them, so they could have done it. Just one, or together."

"But who is left?" said Betty. "You know what Holmes said, 'If you eliminate all the curious incidents, it must be a dog in the nighttime.'"

"But there isn't a dog," said Megan. "Not for thirty years."

Abigail said, "Betty has a point. We have eliminated some of them. So I started to think who would have had access to the murder weapon and might know about the priest hole. Then I knew."

"But any of them could have grabbed the toasting fork. It was right in front of them. And they were all on their own at times, so could have taken it without anyone seeing," said Terry.

"Not that weapon. The one that killed Samuel. That was a spur-of-the-moment decision. Whoever was chasing him had to improvise. Going from behind, unless you have a knife, the best option is strangulation."

"I sometimes worry about you," said Terry. "Are you sure you weren't a serial killer in a past life?"

"Not the last one, but you never know. I did have a sewing customer who was always moaning, so I did think about leaving a pin in one of the hems after coating it with something nasty. Not deadly, just something like itching powder from the seeds inside rose hips or hawthorns."

"I'd hate to get on your bad side. I'm beginning to have second thoughts about our engagement," said Terry.

"You'll be fine. You're already dead. And you're usually on my bad side. Anyway, as I said, the murder weapon used was something long and easy to get hold of and an inch and a bit wide. A bag strap? More likely a belt. The two girls were in leggings, and I asked Megan when I got here what the others were wearing that night. She said Rachel had a loose dress on and the two landladies were wearing straight dresses. I know that Luke had a belt on, and that was threaded through his jeans. I think the chances of him undoing the buckle, pulling it out while crouched over going through the passage are small. But then I thought of a person who had the perfect weapon to hand. Could that person have known about the priest hole? Yes, absolutely. Hayley gave me that information. And would that person be worried if Tyler's secret got out? You bet. That person would lose everything. Job, home, money and, worst of all, someone they loved very much."

"So Luke or Damien," said Lillian.

"I don't think so. Now there is one person who we know had finished with someone a few years ago."

They followed Abigail's eyes as she looked over at the bar where Johnson was chatting happily with Emma. Hayley pointed to the bar for Tom.

"Of course, Louise," said Terry. "She lost her fiancé, so now we know why; she cheated."

"Not Louise. Emma."

Chapter 18

"That's what Tom went to check," said Abigail. "To see if an Emma Lockhart had ever stayed at the Kings Arms Hotel in Amersford. And she had, with a Cameron Brown. Who I seem to remember was Louise's boyfriend. I think they broke up after that and she had no idea why. Neither of them would have wanted to admit their affair to Louise. They knew they'd never be forgiven. Especially as soon after that Emma went into business with her sister. Louise wanted a fresh start. Or maybe the plan was to buy a pub with Cameron to start with."

"That does make sense, hun."

"When Emma saw the look on Tyler's face, she knew just what he meant. We'll never know what made him recall it that night. Something triggered it. Louise made no secret she had lost the love of her life, perhaps she mentioned the name Cameron. This is only a guess, but we can check. It came back to him because he had stayed there the same night with Mia. And it brought back a memory of them being in the bar or at breakfast. Whether he was saying it for fun or blackmail, we'll never know now."

"I can see all that, and the fact that Emma had put a lot of money into the pub, but she said she didn't know about the secret room," said Lillian.

"I don't think she did until recently. But this is where Hayley helped. She learned that business had been slow and they got rid of the cleaner, and Emma said she had to take over the cleaning and she had to polish all the wood. I think she somehow pressed the lever and the panel opened. For whatever reason, she didn't tell her sister, but then we know she can be a bit sneaky."

"What about the murder weapon then?" said Betty. "The belt, I mean."

"And the other clue you said. The running water, hun."

"That's where my glamorous assistant, Suzie, helped. We went up to check some things. Now, the doctor said the thing used to strangle Samuel was four centimetres—that's one and a quarter inches for the oldies. Emma told Johnson she went up to bed with Louise and she put on her dressing gown and read her book. Now unless it's like a granny one—sorry, Betty—it usually has a belt you tie. So that's what we were looking for, wasn't it, Suzie?"

"Abigail thought it might be in the wash, but I found it under the bed behind some boxes."

"It was covered in chalk and dust, so that brings me to the next clue. There was running water on Luke's tape and, even if Emma had worn gloves, she would still have had to wash her hands and arms. Betty, you said your daughter was covered in dirt after her night in the shed. We checked and her bathroom is right above Luke's room."

"Amazing, hun. But why the rush to get over here? Do you think she's going to kill Louise now? I know they say killing gets easier every time."

"Actually, I think Louise is planning on killing Emma. Especially after you told me what was said when you were here with Lady Caroline."

"You'll have to remind me."

Abigail said, "When we first came and met Louise she was so nice. But you said you didn't like her at all as she was rude. And she said something like, 'I'm sure whoever did it will get punished'. So why the change of personality, Hayley? If she hadn't told the police what she guessed, perhaps she had her own vengeance planned. How did Louise know it was her sister? If Emma saw the way Tyler looked at her then probably Louise did. Maybe she remembered the next day that she had seen a receipt in Cameron's wallet for the Kings Arms. That could have been the reason they broke up. I think to start with she just thought, like we did, that Tyler was talking to the ghost hunters about cheating. But perhaps she started to work it out. She might have heard her sister leaving and going downstairs. I don't think Louise thought her sister was a murderer straightaway, but the more the police told her, the more she realised it was her. I'm glad Louise didn't have the chance to take her revenge on Emma. Not for Emma's sake, but for her own. Why should she go to prison? I'd quite like to accidentally push her down those cellar steps myself." After seeing the look on Terry's face, she added, "Not that I would, of course."

Hayley said, "I think you're right. Look at the stare Louise is giving Johnson. I think his arrival might have saved Emma's life. There's an awful lot of hate coming from that direction."

Betty said, "God help the sister that comes between me and my man. That was a song in my day."

"The Beverley Sisters," said Terry.

"When you two Golden Oldies have finished, what are we going to do next?" asked Abigail.

Hayley finished telling Tom and he nodded to where he thought Abigail might be and walked over to talk to his boss at the bar.

"Johnson isn't going to be happy. He's getting very friendly with her," said Lillian.

"Could I have a word, please, sir?"

"No, you can't. I'm off duty, can't you see? You can buy me a beer," and he nodded to Louise behind the bar.

Tom bent down and whispered in his ear.

"You've got to be joking. Come with me, Bennett." They saw him drag the poor constable by the arm into the car park.

"Oh dear," said Hayley. "He's never grateful, is he?"

"We'd better keep our eye on the two sisters," said Abigail, and she got Suzie to move closer to them.

But more customers had arrived and neither Emma nor Louise knew that someone had worked out the truth.

Five minutes later, a red-faced Johnson walked briskly into the bar.

"Emma Lockhart, I'm arresting you on suspicion of the murder of Tyler Drayton and Samuel Brooksby. You do not have to say anything, but it may harm your defence if you do not mention, when questioned, something which you later rely on in court."

Hayley, Louise and all the ghosts watched as Emma was led by Tom to a waiting police car that had arrived to take her to Gorebridge Police Station.

Terry looked up and saw a single crow sitting on the gibbet, its beady eyes watching as well. He remembered the full version of the legend of the black crows.

Three for a death
Two for revenge
And one for a hanging.

Chapter 19

Life in Becklesfield went back to its normal slow pace after the murders in Grimbles Cross were solved. Mrs Merry put out the flowers and opened her shop every day, the bells of St Mary's rang on Sunday, and The Cricketers was busier than ever now the children were back at school.

In Grimbles Cross, three families had had their lives ruined by one throwaway remark. Rachel Drayton was left to bring up her son on her own, while the Brooksbys would have to carry on without theirs, and the doors of The Three Crows had opened again after a closure for 'personal reasons'. There would be one less landlady and one less residential ghost. Morton Glasspool at last felt that he could leave. It was the right time to go in search of his wife and children, hoping for forgiveness and comfort in death.

Emma Lockhart had been charged and had pleaded not guilty to both murders. She was in prison awaiting trial and lived her life in fear of the other prisoners. But not just them. She often caught sight of a menacing dark shadow in her cell. She knew it was Samuel or Tyler—she didn't know why, but she did. She told her lawyer that she wanted to change her plea to guilty, hoping the spectre would leave her alone. Samuel never did, even though his grandmother begged him to move on. Tom told Hayley that in her statement, Emma admitted she was in love with Louise's boyfriend, Cameron, and pursued him until they began an affair, culminating in a stay at the hotel in Amersford. Cameron was filled with guilt, but for Emma's sake he didn't tell Louise the real reason for the breakup. He knew he would never be forgiven and realised he probably hadn't felt enough love for Louise if he had slept with her sister. To take her mind off her broken heart, Louise had begged Emma to help her rebuild her life and open a pub together.

The night of Tyler Drayton's murder, Emma realised straightaway who he was accusing of cheating. He looked her in the eye for a second and she remembered that he had been with a girl who looked a lot like Mia, who was there too. The four of them had chatted at the bar, not knowing none of them should be there. Emma decided she couldn't let him tell Louise. She had more to lose than if she threatened to tell his wife. Rachel was more likely used to his philandering ways. Whether he was after money or something else, she didn't know and didn't care.

Since Emma had started the cleaning, she had noticed how sharp the toasting fork was, so it was an obvious choice as any of the guests that night could have taken it. She took it before she went upstairs for the night. Her dress was loose and, as long as Louise went up the stairs in front of her, no one would notice what she had hidden underneath.

Her luck improved when she heard Drayton's wife leave. Emma crept into his room, expecting him to be asleep. But he was awake and even smiled to see it was her in her nightclothes. He was hoping for a different kind of payment. That made ramming the weapon in even easier. He looked genuinely shocked, she wrote. She hadn't banked on the whole thing being filmed, so she gathered his equipment and crept to the secret room. Emma had pulled on a loose piece of wood when she was polishing the fireplace a few weeks before and decided to keep it to herself. There could be something of value hidden in there that she wanted to check first. Living in the pub for so long, she knew which were the creaky steps and floorboards. What she never expected was for there to be a light in the tunnel. The young Brooksby boy was looking right at her, although she was blinded and didn't know who it was at first. She had just got rid of one blackmailer, so she wasn't going to put up with another one. He had to die as well. But she did feel guilty until she realised it must have been Samuel who had been stealing their stock.

After cleaning herself up, Emma got back into bed. All the pub was quiet and Louise hadn't seemed to hear anything. The pub was full of suspects and no one would think it was her. It was quite exciting, she thought, and would get plenty of customers in. Her only worry was if anyone else knew about the tunnel. Had Samuel told anyone, she wondered. But not even Calum said anything, and she knew they were friends. So she was shocked when that young constable found the priest hole and knew how it opened. That's when she felt an unseen force was working against her.

But something about Louise had changed. Emma couldn't be sure, but her sister's attitude towards her was different. A few looks, an odd remark, and she knew Louise was beginning to suspect her.

Emma thought back to when they were in their teenage years, when jealousies and rivalries had often ended in violence. The statement ended when Emma was in the bar as PC Tom Bennett had come for a meal in The Crows while DCI Johnson was there. Emma Lockhart wrote, "Louise looked at me with such hate that I decided I needed to do something that night. I had to make a run for it, or perhaps Louise could have an accident in the cellar, or an overdose after I planted my dressing gown in her room. I could swear it was hers that had been used to strangle young Samuel. It was going to be me or her. I still had the scar on my arm from when Toby Cash fancied me more when we were on a school trip. As it happened, fate again conspired, and after talking to his constable, Johnson arrested me. In some ways, I was glad to be leaving The Three Crows. It had always had an atmosphere, and since I had taken two lives, I felt a darkness like never before. Even when I killed Tyler I felt like it wasn't me. Had an evil spirit taken over my mind? I hope for some redemption from the living and the dead now that I have confessed."

Abigail was especially pleased that the truth was finally out. There was always a chance that a jury would see the case differently. After all, there was only circumstantial evidence. No one had seen her murder anyone. And there were plenty of people it could also have been. But now they could all get on with their lives again—or their deaths, in the case of the ghosts in the coaching inn and the library.

However, Abigail was bored and hoped there would be another case soon. Not that she wished someone would be brutally murdered, but it would be nice. Terry had taken her to the seaside again, but she missed the excitement and challenge of an investigation.

Eventually, she saw Hayley walk into the library with Benjie and also a big smile on her face. They had a case.

Hayley was disappointed that only Abigail and Betty were there. The others would have loved this one. Not a murder, but a mystery. She joined them at the back and put Benjie on her lap to pretend to be reading him a book.

"No doubt you were getting bored and tetchy, Abigail."

"Not at all. You know me—happy-go-lucky."

Betty tutted and said, "She's been as miserable as a wet hen in a thunderstorm. No wonder the others have said they've got things to do, people to see."

"Rubbish. I've been my normal cheerful self. So come on, Hayley, what's happened?"

"Do you remember I told you that Philip Gowdy told Caroline he wanted to talk to me about a photo?"

"Philip. Wasn't he the one who did the photography at the wedding and helped us solve the case?" said Betty.

"That's him. He's done a lot of jobs for Caroline's charities since then, and he somehow heard about what I do—well, what we do. I've just got off the phone with him and he told me about a photo he took in Ridgeway Wood. He takes shots of birds all over Europe, actually, and while he was in the woods, he got some great ones of a willow warbler. But looking through them when he got home, there were three he'd taken seconds apart that showed something strange."

"Ooh, exciting," said Abigail, sitting forward.

"It wasn't close, but on the right, he could make out there was a hand on a bow with an arrow pulled back ready to fire."

Betty frowned. "I do hope someone wasn't firing at a deer or a rabbit. People are so cruel. I'd like to fire an arrow up their…"

"Ah, hang on though, Betty, I haven't finished. On the left was a silhouette. And it wasn't an animal. It showed someone walking away, and the arrow was pointed right at their back. Philip said you couldn't tell if it was a man or a woman—either of them. He didn't hear anything at the time, but he's got a top-of-the-range camera, so it could have been fifty feet away."

"But wouldn't we have heard something on the news? So either they missed or were just messing around."

"Or," said Abigail, "they haven't found the body yet. Surely you can't just go and buy a deadly weapon like that."

"I'll have a look on my phone," said Hayley. "Here it is: *'It is not illegal to own a bow and arrow in the UK. There are no licensing requirements or age restrictions. However, it is illegal to discharge a bow and arrow in a public place. Hunting animals is prohibited.'* Philip's been checking the news in case someone was missing, but nothing yet. He even took the photo to the police station, but they couldn't do much about it. They said they have enough crimes without possible ones. And they thought the shape on the left could be a tree stump or a bush."

"In other words, the police weren't interested—but I am," said Abigail, standing up. "I'm thinking our Benjamin looks so gorgeous today that he should go and have his photograph taken!"

Chapter 20

Luckily, there was a parking space outside Philip Gowdy Photography in the high street in Boxford. But it still took Hayley four tries to reverse and line up her little Mini with the pavement. Abigail told her she now knew why she had such a small car. Hayley had rung ahead and booked a session for later that day.

"Come on in, Hayley. This must be little Benjamin. He's a little cutie. We'll get some great memories for you to keep."

"I'm sure you will. Tom's always said about having some professional shots done. Otherwise, they just stay on your phone, don't they? Although I've got about a thousand of them."

"Most people have. It's hard to press that delete button, isn't it? I've got some great props we can use."

Abigail told her to ask about the photograph first.

"That would be great, Philip, but I must admit that your telephone call had me intrigued."

"Would you like to see the photo I took?"

"Please," said Hayley.

"You can keep that one if you like. See, all you can see are the hands on the bow. And there's the other figure. The police said it could be a tree stump or a bush. I don't think so."

"It's a person, I can tell. I'm a bit of a psychic, actually."

"I thought you might be," said Philip, with half a smile. "I was talking to Maria about it—that's my wife—and she said there's a lady called Hayley Moon who solves mysteries. I said I was sure that was who came with Lady Caroline. Apparently, you helped a friend of hers to find her inheritance."

"Amanda Calavetti. That's right."

"But I knew you as Bennett."

"That's right too, but if I'm doing anything supernatural or odd, I use Moon. Less awkward for Tom—if you remember him from the wedding."

"I do, the policeman."

"So, what day did you take this photo?"

"It was Friday before last. I try to keep one day free for me. Weekends are always busy with weddings and christenings."

"Do you get some good shots in Ridgeway?"

"Sometimes. I go all over the place. A couple of weeks ago, I went to the coast in Essex. They've got some great bird sanctuaries on the marshes, especially on the Blackwater. But I do like going to Ridgeway Wood."

"Is there anywhere in particular, or do you just walk around?"

"Sometimes. But there are some hides we can use."

"Hides?"

"Basically, they're like wooden sheds with windows on three sides. Not just for birds. They have them for watching badgers or foxes as well."

"I've never seen them," admitted Hayley.

"They can be well hidden and have been there for years, most of them. I daresay some are overgrown now," said Philip. "I've got a map of them if you want it. See this one? I was near there when I took the photo."

"Do you think it could be kids mucking about? I read that anyone can buy a bow and arrow."

"That's right. It's crazy. But thankfully, you have to be eighteen to buy a crossbow. They should be banned. If it was a kid aiming at animals, I'd still like to know who it was. Perhaps the police would do something then."

"And from my experience, Philip, today's bird or animal killer could be tomorrow's serial killer. Being a child is no excuse. Have you got children?"

"A girl, Jessica. She's all grown up now, so I have more time for my hobbies. And I do manage to sell some of my shots if I get a good one."

"I know Lady Caroline was very pleased with hers. I've told her I want one of the calendars from the gymkhana."

"Birds and horses; they're my favourites. Sorry, perhaps I should say babies."

"That's okay. But I'd love to look into it for you. I work with some other people who can help. It's a strange case, but we've had stranger ones."

"Really? Right, I've got someone else at five, so I'll go and set the shoot up."

Hayley turned to see Abigail and Betty about to walk through the shop front. "We'll see you later, Hayl, we're off to Ridgeway Wood."

Chapter 21

WHILE BENJAMIN WAS PUT IN A VARIETY OF COSTUMES and hats, which left him totally confused, Abigail and Betty had started up the main path through nearby Ridgeway Wood. It was quieter than at the weekend, which pleased them. It got a bit tedious having someone pass through you.

"I don't know how we can find the hides without the map, Betty. They seemed to be spread all over the place."

"I know where two of them are. When John and I were courting we liked to go there and..."

"Thank you, Betty, I can imagine."

"I was going to say kiss. We were courting, not married. It was a different age then. But you're right, if we were married we would have loved to have got back to nature, shall we say."

Betty and John had what Betty had called a saucy marriage. Even after death, she'd had more gentlemen's advances than Abigail. There was Willy Morgan at Ottersmill Marina and Sir Timothy Whittlebury at the Courtridge Hotel.

"There's one up this fork to the left. It's well hidden, that's why we liked it," said Betty.

There was a small clearing, and Abigail saw a wooden cabin

with a door on one side and small viewing windows on the others. There were no birdwatchers in there, or even any birds to be watched. A bench was the only seating, and there were window sills under the hatches where Abigail thought they would rest their binoculars, notebooks and cameras.

"Not many home comforts, Betty."

"It seemed bigger and more romantic in our day, I must admit."

"You never thought about being a twitcher and watching the birds?" asked Abigail.

"I was more of a curtain-twitcher," laughed Betty.

"Me too, Betty. The lesser-crested Karen Gibbs' mating rituals at number twenty-four were far more interesting. Well, I can't recognise any trees from the photo. Shall we go and look for another one? I'm rather jealous of you and John. I wasn't even in a relationship for a year."

"We had over sixty together, dear."

"I don't think anyone could have put up with me for that long. And nor me with them. But even for eternity, Terry is looking a pretty good bet. Shame my mum can't see me now."

"How do you know she can't? We've seen others come and go."

"That's true. She'd like him. So would Dad."

Betty slid her arm through Abigail's. "You deserve happiness, dear. You're very thoughtful and kind, and you'd do absolutely anything for anyone. I know there are some people who say that you're a bit bossy, opinionated, terribly big-headed…"

"Thank you, Betty, that's enough compliments for one day," said Abigail, hoping they would find something before she got even more depressed.

After backtracking and going up another fork, they saw another bird hide.

"Oh yes, this was our favourite. When the moon rose it would be right over that clump of trees. Happy times."

"I don't think I'd want to sit there for hours doing nothing," said Abigail.

"Oh, we were doing something, dear."

"I was talking about Philip and the others, Betty," laughed Abigail. "You must have been a cheap date. I should imagine Terry would have brought me somewhere like this in the real world. He would have said it's far more romantic than a weekend away or a fancy meal."

"Well, thriftiness is next to godliness, you know."

"I think you'll find it's cleanliness. And it doesn't look all that clean either."

"If you're in love it doesn't matter where you are, Abigail."

"I know, but I'm saying if I had the choice I wouldn't be in this rickety old hut that's riddled with worms and beetles."

"Oh, and spiders. Let's go," said Betty, getting out quickly.

"I can remember when I first died we came here looking for that man, and we met an old lady who was always here," said Abigail. "She was sitting on a stump with a basket of bluebells. She told us where he was when he died."

"I know the one. She's friends with Terry. I think her name was Rosie. She was actually sitting on the very stump that John carved our names on after we…"

"Oh, God," said Abigail, covering her ears.

"After we got married. Honestly, Abigail, I really think you have a one-track mind."

"Me? You and John were always…"

"There you go again. Don't assume, it makes me an ass, as they say."

"If you say so, Betty."

Luckily, the Victorian lady came into view. She was walking down the path towards them. Abigail did wonder how she was holding a basket of flowers at the exact time of death. Maybe she was selling them, or picking them in the bluebell meadow in Ridgeway Wood. But she wasn't in the mood for going down memory lane today—only the one that led to another possible victim.

"Good day, ladies. No Terry today?"

"He's showing some newly Deads around Frimble."

"If I was a hundred years younger I'd be after that man. He's so kind and thoughtful."

"He's spoken for now, Rosie. Abigail here has caught his eye."

"You? That does surprise me. But they say opposites attract."

"And what is that supposed to mean? Are you saying…"

Betty decided to intervene. "Have you seen anyone going round with a bow and arrow?"

"Like Robin Hood, you mean?"

"Not exactly. It would have been about seven or eight days ago."

"Not that I can remember. I saw a woman on a bike, showing all her legs. Er, a man with a shotgun one night about two weeks ago. He was after an old fox, so I scared him off and led the poor fox into an old shed."

"How did you scare the man off?" Abigail wanted to know.

"I've got a few tricks up my sleeve. Let's just say I've become one with the wood. If I get angry, it does. A sudden whirlwind of leaves and branches blocking your way can be overpowering for anybody."

"Love it," said Abigail. "Serves him right for chasing a poor little fox. Hang on, did you say an old shed? Is it near here?"

"Not far. No living person goes in there anymore. So I knew the little mite would be safe there until he went back to his family. I'll show you."

It wasn't one that Betty had seen, and it was a long walk for them. Abigail just hoped it would be worth it. And it was.

No Breather, as Terry called them, could have got in there easily. But there was a portion of the undergrowth that had been flattened. Abigail went in expecting the worst.

There was a Breather in there. But this one was no longer breathing. Face down in the narrow hide was a body amongst the moss and weeds. A young woman dressed in a cream gilet had a small hole in her back, which Abigail and Betty guessed had been made by an arrow.

Chapter 22

"So how much is that going to cost us?" Tom wanted to know.

"It depends how many we buy. And you're always saying you wanted to get some professional shots of our son."

"When have I ever said that? I've got four pictures of me as a baby. We take more than that in an hour. And you're expecting me to pay twenty pounds for one?"

"Twenty? It'll be more than that, hun, I'm afraid."

"Why don't you just go the whole hog and get some done of the cat?"

"Good idea. He does lovely ones of pets."

"I was joking, don't you dare, Hayley."

"Look, I've got a couple of them on my phone. Philip put Benjie on a stool in a little panda costume with cute little ears."

"How ridiculous… Oh, he's adorable," said the proud daddy. "And he's got a ladybird outfit in this one. You can have one. Three, five max. Actually, Luna would look cute in a sailor outfit."

"You've changed your tune. We've taken some nice ones, but

they aren't with him posing like that. He's usually eating or playing."

"Mum will definitely want one. And your parents. And we'd better get one for his godmother, Janine."

One smile from his son and he had caved in. A bit like he did after one purr from Luna. Tom was a policeman, but he was soft as a marshmallow in the middle, thought Hayley, and she loved him for it.

"What do you want for tea, hun?"

A cold breeze filled the room as if a spirit or two had entered the room. Any kind thoughts that Tom had had about Abigail were gone. "She's back, isn't she?"

"Give me one minute and I'll get rid of her, I promise."

Hayley took a minute but did not get rid of her. She went back in sheepishly and sat down next to him. Tom ignored her and put the football on. He had a bad feeling about her arrival.

"Er, hun, what if I told you there was a body in Ridgeway Wood?"

"I'd say tell me after I've had my tea and the match is finished. I'll have scampi and chips."

"Are you serious, Tom?"

"Deadly. Whoever it is isn't going to be any less dead in a couple of hours. If you were normal I wouldn't even know."

"Normal? That's so…"

"True? Ask her if it's just happened?"

"I know it's been there over a week."

"In that case, there's no rush. In fact, it's going to be dark soon, so we'll think of a reason to find the body in the morning. Forensics won't be happy if they have to work in the dark. You never know, someone else might find it with a bit of luck. Plenty of chips." Tom pretended to be nonchalant about the body, but he did feel guilty. He didn't even want to ask if it was a man or a woman. But he could just imagine the trouble if he made Johnson leave The Red Lion.

Hayley joined Abigail and Betty in the kitchen and turned the oven on.

"So, it's a girl or a woman. How awful for her family."

"I'd say she's in her early twenties. She had lovely dark, wavy hair, but it was tangled with twigs. You couldn't see much of her face. The hole in her back had dried blood that had trickled downwards."

"Bless her, that means she was probably upright for a while after she was shot. She must have started running away."

"That's dreadful," said Betty. "Does that mean she took herself there, or was she dragged or carried?"

"It makes a difference," said Abigail. "Either the victim or the killer knew about the hide. Forensics will be able to work it out. They need to get there. If you've got that map off Philip, I'll show you which one it is."

"Listen, I know this is going to sound very bad, but it's nearly dark and no one is going to be able to do anything till the morning. Why should Tom go without a night's sleep just because I'm not normal. I'm sorry, Abigail, you'll have to wait."

"But I agree, Hayley. Honestly, why do people think I'm some kind of tyrant? Even the old lady in the woods said something like that. I'm the nicest person you could ever meet, aren't I, Betty?"

"You are, dear. Well, not ever, but in the top ten, maybe top hundred anyway."

"Thank you, Betty. If you stick up for me any more, I might have to kill myself if I wasn't already dead."

Hayley laughed. "Well, I think it's very lovely of you, hun. And we've got to think of how Tom could know. I hate how he has to lie so much."

"Exactly. It's right in the far part of the woods. You'd never see it from the path."

Betty had an idea that wasn't far from the truth. "He could say he was going to the car when he saw an old lady. And she says she was picking flowers and stumbled across it. Then she could leave before Tom had the chance to get her full name. He'd even pass a lie detector because it's nearly true."

"I don't think it would come to that, but it is a good idea and only a tiny lie."

"He's just leaving the messenger out," said Abigail. "And you know what they did to them in the past."

"I know what he'd like to do to you at the moment. Especially if I don't put his tea on. So we're agreed, he'll tell the station in the morning. Let's hope it's Johnson's day off."

Chapter 23

"What do you mean Bennett said there's a body in a birdwatching cabin in Ridgeway Wood?" shouted DCI Johnson.

"An elderly lady told him as he was leaving for work. She'd been picking flowers near there. But she wouldn't give her address, only that her name was Rosie," said Sergeant Mills. "We know roughly where it is. Shall I take some uniforms and look?"

"Yes, and take Bennett with you."

"Funny thing is, sir, we had a report that someone was seen with a bow and arrow near there, and we dismissed it."

"That's not going to please the CC if the press gets hold of it. You'd better get going. And don't forget your boots."

It was muddy there, and Tom was glad that he kept his wellingtons in the car. Hayley had sent him the map of the bird and badger hides, which he told Mills he had downloaded from the internet. He suggested which one they should check first. His friend had a funny feeling that Tom knew more than he was saying, but didn't want to know.

They could tell they had the correct place as soon as they got close. What Abigail and Betty hadn't known was that there was a horrific smell of decomposition that led the police to the hide, which was covered by stinging nettles and bushes. Abigail realised as soon as she saw Mills covering his nose.

Betty felt for Abigail's hand and felt so sorry for the poor girl and her family. Lillian had gone to see what she could deduce as a nurse and followed Tom in.

"Your old lady was right, Tom. It's dreadful. I don't think we had a missing person report for her, do you?"

"No, Dave. I wonder why. Looks like she's been here a few days."

"Put the tape up, we'll wait outside. I don't suppose the old woman told Hayley who she is?"

Tom looked guilty and gave a wry smile. "Unfortunately not. But she did think it had something to do with the bow and arrow report."

"We'll leave that up to the doctor to tell us first. Could even be a bullet hole. But I'm sure this girl's family are happy that your wife has so many friends even if Johnson isn't. In fact, I'd say it's quite remarkable, actually, and good on them."

"Somebody loves us," said Betty.

They listened while Mills phoned Johnson, and they could hear him shouting even though he wasn't on loudspeaker. He told him to leave two constables to watch the crime scene and get back to the station. "And take that daft Bennett with you."

The three spirits decided to get back to Becklesfield. Hayley put Benjie down for his nap and caught up with the sad details.

"Sorry, Hayley, we didn't feel we could stay and watch like we usually do. I feel really upset with this one for some reason."

"It's maternal, hun. You could be her mum, and a young person's death is always more upsetting."

Lillian added, "And the condition of the body made it so much worse, Hayley. I'm so glad you weren't there to see it."

Abigail said, "I can't see a young girl like that knowing where birdwatchers go, so we ought to ask Philip who might. Surely there can't be that many people interested in bird-watching around here."

"I'll give him a ring. I'm sure he won't mind. He should be told that the police are taking notice of the photo now and will probably be round to see him soon."

Philip was pleased, but devastated to learn that if he had seen it with his eyes he might have been able to prevent the death. And he guessed there could be as many as two hundred people over the years who knew about it.

"You're kidding? We'll never be able to narrow it down," Hayley told him.

"You could start with the BLBs."

"Sorry? I have no idea what that is."

"The Becklesfield Loves Birds club. I thought you lived there."

"I do, but I've never heard of it." Neither had any of the others. "There can't be many members. Where do they meet?"

"Probably about fifty members, but they don't all go. I only went once, and there were only about ten there. It was held at the town hall. But they would all have got a map of the woods."

"Would you have a list of the members? Or do you know who would?"

"I know the chairman is Harold Harding. I could give you his number."

"That's okay, Philip, I know him quite well. He runs the charity shop here. If you talk to anyone, can I ask you not to mention that we've spoken? Or even that you know me. It could complicate things because I'm married to a policeman."

"I understand. Thanks for giving me a heads-up that they'll

want to talk to me. By the way, they hold a meeting every second Monday of the month, so it will be on next week."

"I'll pop and see Mr Harding first. I wonder if he'll suddenly believe I've taken an interest in birds."

"Probably not, Hayley. Numbers are dwindling. You can get a live feed on the internet now from home. Especially for the badgers. Saves all that waiting around in freezing weather in the dark."

"Are there ones with cameras in Ridgeway?"

"No, it's old school there, unfortunately. And real photographers want to be the ones that get the perfect shot."

"Well, thank you for your help, Philip. Don't forget, if someone called Johnson mentions my name, you've never heard of me. Speak soon. Bye."

"We'd better get you a camera then if you're joining the BLB," laughed Abigail.

"I'm not standing knee-deep in the rain and mud filming birds, hun."

"It's all in the dry, dear. I was telling Abigail how I would be laying on my back with John…"

"Betty!"

"I was going to say looking at the moon and stars. Honestly, you two only think of one thing."

"Sorry, hun. But I was going to say that I could go and see Mr Harding at Wet & Wildlife and say I want to donate some money for the birds or something. The charity gives all its profits to Ridgeway Wood and the River Gore. Then I can ask a few questions about Becklesfield Loves Birds. And maybe even go next week."

"It's funny," said Terry. "That meant something completely different in my day."

Abigail gave him one of her looks. "What have I told you about calling us birds?"

"I don't see the problem. Birds are nice."

"So are dogs, and we don't want to be called them either."

"Fox?"

"Since you've been dead, ladies have decided they don't want to be called any sort of fauna."

"You called me a cheeky monkey the other day," said Terry.

"That's because you are. Women are allowed to anyway."

"When you two lovebirds are finished," said Hayley.

"Oh, you'd better not call us that anymore," said Terry, looking at Abigail.

"As I was saying," said Hayley, "I'll pop to Wet & Wildlife, but I've also had another idea of what to do. There's another club that we need to check out. There's a possibility that the murderer might be a member of an archery club. That's far more me. I had a go once at a holiday camp and I was rather good. I might not have to do anything with birds, hopefully."

But then Tom rang to tell her that forensics hadn't identified the body yet, but they could tell by the footprints that the girl had been carried to the hide on purpose. Whoever it was knew exactly that it was there.

Chapter 24

"Morning, Mrs Bennett," said Mr Harding. "Have you got another do to go to? We've had some lovely outfits donated this week. My, your little one is growing fast."

"He is. And he's getting heavy."

"It's a lovely age though. Make the most of it. Soon they start giving you backchat and telling you where to go," he laughed.

"Oh dear, I hope not that soon. You've got a teenager, I take it."

"I wish. I've got two. But the girl isn't quite as bad. And she's away at university. The boy is still at home, but he'll grow out of it soon, I hope."

"They usually do. I can't say I was an angel at that age. I haven't had a look at your long skirts for a while. Now I've got Benjie, I seem to spend all the money on him."

Mrs Malloy joined in from the back of the charity shop. "We've got some nearly new baby clothes. And toys."

Hayley went to look. "He grows out of things so fast. I think he's going to be tall like his daddy. I'll definitely have these. I've got some that I could bring in that don't fit him."

"We're always grateful," said Mrs Malloy. "But maybe you should hang on to them. You might have another boy to pass them on to."

Hayley didn't like to say that she already predicted she would be having a girl next time. Hopefully not for about two years. She moved over to look at the toys. She didn't want to lie, but as luck had it she didn't have to. Amongst the toys was a brightly coloured parrot.

"Oh, he'll love this. Look, Benjie, you love birds, don't you?"

Hayley hoped Mrs Malloy wouldn't notice him pointing excitedly at the big grey dinosaur money box next to it. He started grizzling, so she picked that up as well.

"A lady brought the parrot and some men's clothes in yesterday. You press that button and the parrot squawks. But if you press that one, you speak into there and it repeats what you've said, like parrots do. But she said it stopped working. It used to belong to her nephew. So you can have it for five pounds if you like."

"Thank you, that's perfect." Hayley walked over to the till where Harold Harding, chairman of the BLB, was waiting to take the money.

"I was saying to Mrs Malloy that Benjie loves birds. I put him in his chair and he'll sit for ages watching them in the garden. I must get a bird table. I think I have a future birdwatcher in the making."

"That's a coincidence. I'm into that myself. We have a club right here in the village — Becklesfield Loves Birds."

"Really? How come I've never heard of it? Do many people go?"

"Quite a few. That's part of why I volunteer here. The money goes to the birds as well as the foxes and badgers. You'd be surprised what birds you get around here."

"I heard someone say that Ridgeway Wood is a great place to see all sorts. I'd like to take some photos to put in his nursery.

Or get a mural painted on his wall." Hayley was a bit worried about how easily she was telling lies these days. She'd been spending too much time with Abigail. But it was to find a vicious killer.

"We know some great places where you can get some really special shots. You should come to a meeting. Bring Tom or even Benjie if he's not in bed. It's next Monday at seven o'clock in the town hall."

"I might do that. I won't stay long because it's his bedtime."

"We have a cup of tea and a biscuit first, then I can introduce you to everyone," he said as he passed the clothes and the dinosaur to Hayley. Then he bent down to pass the green, yellow and red parrot to Benjamin, who threw it on the floor.

"Whoops, butterfingers. I'll carry it for him. Thank you, Mr Harding. I'll look forward to seeing you on Monday."

When they got outside Abigail said, "And you said you don't lie, Hayley Bennett."

"A little white one for the sake of that girl, hun."

"Just the one?"

"And now I've got to lie to get into an archery club. I wish you could do it."

"I wish I could too," said Abigail sadly.

"I'm sorry, hun. It's hard for you as well. Let's take Benjie to the swings and I'll look on my phone. I can't imagine there's one around here. I'm sure I would have known about that. Surely you've got to have a big space, and somewhere safe so you don't accidentally kill someone."

When Benjie was on his favourite swing, Hayley searched for 'Archery near me'.

"They do it at the local golf club. I did not know that. I suppose they've got the room. It's on every Saturday morning. It's run by Olympic gold medallist Anthea Dart. Well, that's an appropriate name. Reminds me of Damien Shadow. I wonder if hers is real."

"Does she live in Becklesfield?" said Abigail, looking over Hayley's shoulder.

"It doesn't say. I'm sure we would know if she did."

"I wonder if you have to be a member to go in the golf club for lunch?"

"If you do, I've had it," said Hayley. "They're hardly likely to let the likes of us peasants join. Not that Tom knows which end of a golf club to hold."

"But luckily you know someone who isn't a peasant."

"Oh no, not Lady Caroline again. I'm always asking her for favours."

"She loves it. And don't forget it's her fault you're in this mess. She was the one that gave Philip your number."

"Okay," said Hayley wearily. "I'll ring her, again."

Chapter 25

HAYLEY HAD A DECISION TO MAKE: WHETHER SHE should park her little Mini next to the Porsche or the Range Rover SUV. She decided the latter, because it would partially hide it from the golfers who were making their way to the first tee.

As she sat in the car checking her make-up in the mirror, the owner lifted his clubs into the back and peered down at the woman in the old car. He wondered what she was doing there. He didn't need to say anything for her to know that he was dying to tell her that it was for members only. Hayley wished she could have said she was there with a member of the aristocracy, but neither said anything and just gave the other a look — one of disdain and one of dislike.

Lady Caroline was already there and had ordered their drinks. The clubhouse was a converted manor house which had once belonged to the De Fleur family. It wasn't a hotel but held functions like weddings and conferences. Inside it was modern and airy, unlike most of the big houses that Hayley had been in lately.

"I'm so sorry to ask another favour, Caroline."

"You're joking. I love all this cloak-and-dagger stuff. To think that a photo I saw helped to find the body of a girl. I'm so pleased I can do something to help. My life has been a lot more interesting since I met you and the others. Are they present?"

"No, thank goodness. I told them I wanted you and I to have a normal conversation. It's so hard when someone is chattering in your ear. Is the murder on the news yet? I haven't had a chance to look."

"Yes," said Caroline. "On television and online. It's very sad. They're asking for help to identify her."

"Tom said he'd let me know as soon as they do. She had no bag or identification with her. But the killer could have thrown that anywhere in the wood and it would probably never be found. And at her age I don't suppose she's ever had her fingerprints or DNA taken."

"Surely someone would have noticed her missing — her parents or friends."

"They are checking. The trouble is she might not be from around here. May not even be from England. And if she had left home, who knows if anyone had noticed. Poor thing. I've got Philip's photo if you want to have a look, Caroline."

"Please. I did have a quick look at it on his phone, but this is better. Although you can't tell if it's a man or a woman, can you?"

"Not by the hands. Although they think she was carried or dragged to where she was found, chances are it's a man. Or a strong woman, at any rate."

"What about the figure? I suppose we know that's a girl now."

"I hope so, Caroline. We don't want there to be two victims. Going by the legs, I'd say she's walking, not running."

"She doesn't even know that someone is about to take her life."

"But that doesn't mean she wasn't with him. They might

have gone there to have a bit of fun, shooting at trees or something. Perhaps I could get Abigail and the others to look for holes in the bark. But it's a long shot, excuse the pun. Philip has been asked to take them to where he thinks he took the photo."

"Could it be an accident, Hayley?"

"Stranger things, hun. But why didn't the shooter get her help instead of hiding the body?"

Caroline took a sip of her white wine. "So what are we doing here?"

"Before I tell you, I want to know about Jasper. Have you had your second date? And where did he take you this time? Paris, Vienna?"

"Brentwood."

"Brentwood?!" said Hayley. "Do you mean the one in Essex, or is there one in the south of France?"

"No, the one in Essex. After the helicopter date I was quite pleased. He wanted to show me where he was born. His rags-to-riches story. It was rather enjoyable actually. We found a lovely pub in the country."

"And?"

"And we had a gorgeous meal and then we came home."

"Well, we can't say he's not the perfect gentleman," said Hayley.

"I wouldn't say that," smiled Caroline. "What if I told you that he likes bacon and egg for breakfast."

"I'd say good for you, hun. It's about time you had some happiness. I think this could become something really good for both of you. I expect to be kept up with all the juicy gossip. I feel responsible for the pair of you."

"I promise, Hayley. Now I know you didn't ask me here just to find out about my love life, so what are we here for?"

"Who better to fire a bow and arrow with that accuracy than someone that does it regularly? There must be someone we can ask about archery. They do it here on a Saturday."

"I know. They rent the land on the other side of the Pitch and Putt. Colonel Walsh is over there. He always is at lunchtime; it gets him away from Mrs Walsh. There's not much that he doesn't know about what goes on here. Trouble is, if we ask him we probably won't be able to get away. I heard someone say that he can talk for hours on a subject he knows nothing about. Apparently, he fought for England and now he talks for England."

"Very handy in our line of work, hun."

"As long as you're not paying your babysitter by the hour."

Luckily Hayley wasn't, as Colonel Walsh spent the first half-hour talking about his service to Queen Elizabeth, then the next on his golf handicap. Although Caroline did tell Hayley afterwards that she had never seen him with a golf club in his hand, only a pint of Guinness. Eventually, she was able to bring the subject back to archery.

"Funnily enough I competed in the Indoor Interservices Army Championship myself. Got down to the last two. That was years ago, though. Don't think my eyes are good enough these days. Or my right arm," he said, lifting his drink. "These bows take a lot of strength. Did you know that archaeologists can tell who was a longbowman by the size and shape of the shoulder joints? Or by the wrist guards, of course. I'm a bit of an expert on Agincourt."

"Fascinating," said Hayley, wondering how she could get the conversation back to the present day. "So you know about bows then. I've got a photo of one here. Would you be able to tell us about the make and who is likely to own it?"

"I know one thing, if you're serious about it they can cost a fortune. Let me see then. Rum sort of photograph." The colonel put on his metal-rimmed glasses and held it close to his eyes. "No real archer I know would use that. Tell a lie, I do know someone. I bought my grandson one for his thirteenth birthday. It's just a regular recurve bow that anyone can use."

"So no archer here would own one?"

"No, Lady Caroline. The modern ones have stabilisers with weights, amongst other things. This is just a plain old wooden bow you can buy anywhere for not much money. I make sure my grandson only uses it when he comes to our house. We've got an area with a hill behind it in our garden. You can't be too careful. It's not as accurate as a proper bow, but, ladies, it's still deadly in the wrong hands."

Chapter 26

Tom had put Benjie to bed and read him a bedtime story, and was now sitting on the sofa with Hayley on his left and Luna on his lap. The cat would have preferred the woman to go on her own chair, but he soon fell asleep nevertheless.

The autopsy of the young lady had been moved to first in the queue, and although she hadn't been identified, she was thought to be about twenty-one or twenty-two. The murder weapon was determined to be 7.95 millimetres in diameter and had penetrated her right lung and rib cage from the rear. It had been removed shortly after death. The time of death would have occurred about five minutes after the arrow entered the back.

"It's not a hunting arrow; you can't just pull those out. And they think it happened about eight days ago, but need to do more tests," said Tom.

"That fits in with when Philip took the photo," said Hayley.

Tom didn't tell her about the decomposition of the torso and the animal foraging. Not to his empathic wife. He had found it hard enough when he read the report.

"Did they find where the photo was actually taken?"

"Eventually. Your friend was very helpful. With all the twigs and leaves, we didn't get any good casts of footprints."

"Was it near to where she was found?"

"It was if you knew where the hide was. As the crow flies it was only about a hundred yards."

"Don't mention crows again, hun. We've had enough of them lately."

"Oh, yeah," laughed Tom.

"So it would have been a man if he carried her."

"Not necessarily. She could have run towards it. Or he might not have fired the arrow when the picture was taken but nearer to where she was found. There was no sign of blood anywhere."

"You didn't find any other arrows or holes, did you?"

"There's too much shrubbery there. We'd never find them. Johnson wants to get the dogs in."

"What else is he going to do?"

"You know him, he's going to have the photo tested for Photoshop. Just in case the photographer was giving himself an alibi."

"Hadn't even occurred to me. Fair enough, I suppose."

"And we're checking if any shops in Gorebridge sold one of the bows lately."

"They sell them all over the internet as well. He's going to question the birdwatchers, I hope."

"He's asking for dog walkers and anyone else that goes there to get in touch. He won't take any notice of me, Hayley."

"I will then. You can watch Benjie on Monday when I go, can't you?"

"Probably. Watch what you say then if you really think one of them is a killer."

"I will, hun. Right, I'll put the kettle on. I've had enough of murder for one day."

Tom turned the television on and she turned around to watch. Talking right into the camera was an angry-looking man.

"And I'm prepared to offer a twenty-thousand-pound reward to find out whoever did this to our beautiful daughter." He took a deep breath and put his arm around a small woman who was dabbing at her eyes and nose.

The newsreader came on the screen and said, "That is the father of the murder victim who was found in Ridgeway Wood. The body is thought to be that of twenty-four-year-old Felicity Fortescue of Crockley-on-Edge."

"That poor couple," said Tom. "They must have seen the news and recognised her from the descriptions. I'll find out the details tomorrow. I can't believe he's offered a reward already. That's just made extra work for us. He should have given the investigation a chance first."

Hayley was frowning. "I know that man. I can't think where I've seen him. I know. He was the one getting in his Range Rover at the golf club and gave me a dirty look."

"That's a bit of a coincidence. What are the odds of that?"

"Quite low from what I've learned. I might go up, hun. It's a difficult case to process for me," sighed Hayley.

She decided she had to get some things straight in her mind. The fact that a family was now grieving for a daughter was weighing her down. Hayley lit some candles and took a long bath. How she wished she could just ring up her best friend, Abigail, and have a chat. But it wasn't easy when that person was deceased.

She needed to know if it was coincidence or fate that she had met the girl's father. Or providence that meant the archery club was important. Mr Fortescue had looked down on her for not having a fancy car, but Hayley had a feeling that he would soon be looking for her help to get over the worst time of his life.

Chapter 27

IN ANOTHER PART OF BECKLESFIELD, MOLLY TRAVIS had also watched the news. The difference was she hadn't been upset, she was excited. She wondered if that was the day she had taken her Cockapoo to the woods. It was a nice day and she felt like getting away from her mum for a while.

Molly recalled there had been some sort of photographer there. She guessed he was a professional, going by his camera. She'd even smiled at him, hoping he would ask her to model for him. But he seemed more interested in an old tree and a bird. That was until an elderly couple scared it away. She lay in bed trying to think who else was there. They had said it was more than a week ago, so it could be that day. If so, there were three hopefuls there. They hadn't shown a picture of the girl yet, but if she was wearing cream and had long brown hair then she had seen her as well. If that was Felicity Fortescue, she had been on her own, walking quite fast and not carrying a bag. She thought it was a bit strange, her not having a dog that she could see, and being well dressed. It must be something to do with that photographer. She was pretty; maybe he had arranged to meet her there and killed her. It had to be him. Could she describe him though? A bit under six feet, in his fifties, dark hair going a bit grey. Black jacket and jeans. And she would definitely be able to pick him out of a police line-up.

Molly started to think about what she would do with the twenty thousand pounds reward. A car, although she would have to learn to drive first. Or put a deposit on a flat; she could move out then. And she'd definitely leave her boring job.

Then she remembered that was also the day she bumped into her friend, who would know for sure what day it was. She wouldn't mention the money. Just have a casual chat. No, she definitely wouldn't mention the twenty thousand pounds. And she wouldn't mention it to her mum either. She was a born worrier. She would tell her to keep out of it and leave it to the police. And probably say it might put her own life in danger. Her mum always got worked up about nothing. But it would be nice to treat her to afternoon tea somewhere, once she got all that lovely money.

Chapter 28

ALL THE MEMBERS OF THE AGENCY HAD SOMEHOW heard about the girl being identified as Felicity Fortescue and the reward offered. It appeared that village gossip didn't only travel fast for the living.

At Hayley's house in Church Lane, Abigail started off the proceedings.

"So what do we know about the poor girl, Hayley?"

"We know she wasn't poor in one sense. Her family is loaded. She was a bit of a socialite. Fast cars and a fast life. And she posted every day."

"Royal Mail isn't as efficient as it was in my day," said Betty. "Did you know that we had a delivery at seven in the morning, then another one at lunchtime?"

"Those days have gone, hun. But I actually meant she put everything she did on TikTok and things like that, and recorded it all on her phone."

"So that will make it much easier for us then, dear. Where is this Tick Tock?"

"Tom said they've got an officer going through it all, Betty. But there's nothing at all posted on the day of the murder. The last post she did was the night before, saying that she was going to get a surprise on the next day, so that's not much help."

"Getting shot with a bow and arrow in Ridgeway Wood would qualify for that. Or shooting one herself," said Terry.

"But Tom said a lot of her posts were things like saving animals and cute cats."

"What was she dressed in? That might give us a clue," said Suzie.

"Skinny jeans, a cream sports gilet and an expensive pair of trainers. So she wasn't going anywhere she had to be smart. Although the whole outfit probably cost more than my car."

"It could have been an accident if they were just mucking about in the woods," said Suzie. "Although she wasn't walking with anyone in the photo, she could have been walking off in a huff, or she was looking for whoever it was she was meeting."

"I don't think so, hun. Whoever was looking down that shaft would have noticed her. This was no accident. Mills checked and they hadn't met at the coffee shop there."

"We need to talk to one of her friends," said Abigail. "The picture was a bit blurry; maybe she was carrying a bow as well. She might have mentioned it to someone."

"I'm ahead of you, hun. Tom said that one of her besties was Kylie Silver."

"That name rings a bell. Oh, a silver bell."

"That's what I thought. Especially when Tom gave me the address. Do you remember when we were investigating the murder at the regatta, we went to Edenbury Heights?"

"The posh gated community, yes, of course. There was a footballer who lived there with his young family called Silver."

"Marlon. This is his wife. They live next to Heather Lockwood, the TV chef. She might be able to get me in to see her because she knows Caroline well. Kylie would know what Felicity was going to do. I'm just surprised she wasn't worried when all the posts stopped."

"Well, let's get going to Edenbury Heights to find out," said Abigail.

Pulling up at the iron gates at the entrance to Edenbury Heights brought back a lot of memories of their investigation there. As they waited to be let in, Abigail and Terry laughed about when Johnson was chased by a huge dog and jumped on top of his car just in time.

Heather Lockwood had told her neighbour that Hayley had helped her when a good friend of hers had been murdered. When she added that Hayley was also a good friend of Lady Caroline Hatton, that was enough to make the Instagrammer agree to see her.

At the sprawling house, named The Beeches, Kylie Silver opened the door, and Hayley, Abigail and Terry could see her eyes were puffy and red from crying. Yet she had still made sure to apply all her make-up and do her hair to perfection. She was also dressed immaculately, and her sandals echoed on the marble floor as she led Hayley to the sumptuous sofa in the light and spacious lounge.

"Heather said you know Lady Caroline Hatton and help people that are grieving. Are you some kind of therapist?"

"Yes, I am. I specialise in loss and try to help however I can. I'm so sorry this happened to your friend. How long had you known each other?"

"Only about two years, but we clicked right away. We met at a club in London. Fliss was there with one of Marlon's mates. And she doesn't live far from here – well, didn't. We got married last year and she was one of my bridesmaids."

"Weren't you worried when she stopped posting or getting in touch?"

"Fliss was a friend, but she was a fair-weather one. She only got in touch for fun things. If I had any problems, she wouldn't be the one I'd go to. If I wanted to go out on the town, then yes. And if she was struggling she wouldn't have confided in me. And I know that if I wasn't with a famous footballer she wouldn't have given me the time of day. Even if I started talking about my daughter, she'd soon bring the subject back to her. But that was okay."

"Had she gone offline before this?" asked Hayley.

"She could be a bit up and down. If she was depressed, she would go off on her own. She had enough money to fly to the south of France or stay in someone's villa. And I know she'd met a new man, so I assumed she was with him."

"A boyfriend?"

"Yes. But she wouldn't say who he was. Only that he was gorgeous to look at and really nice. And a bit different to her usual ones. Perhaps he didn't want to be plastered all over the internet. Especially if he was married or someone in the public eye."

"So it could be a wife who wanted her dead."

"It wouldn't be the first time. It could even be an ex. There were plenty of them that Fliss had left behind."

"Who was her last one that you know about?"

"That would be Rex Dubois. He's the sporty type. Not football though. He's a tennis player and a champion archer."

"Is he really? You must tell the police, Kylie."

"Why?"

"It's not been released yet, so keep it to yourself, but she was killed by an arrow."

Kylie covered her face. "That's awful. She must have felt it go in and seen it sticking out of her."

"It was in her back, hun."

"How do you know so much? Her dad phoned me and didn't mention that."

"I know someone in Gorebridge police. What did her dad say to you?"

"He demanded to know who she was seeing and what else I knew. I could only say what I told you."

"So he didn't know who this new man was either. I'm thinking if she didn't tell her family it could mean they wouldn't approve of him. Maybe married or a bit dodgy."

Abigail added, "Or even worse: poor."

So Hayley asked, "What if it was someone further down the social scale?" Although she knew the answer to that after her brush with Mr Fortescue at the golf club.

"He's a right snob. Her mum isn't. I have a feeling she wished she had married for love and not money. But her dad wouldn't have approved at all. They loved Rex and hoped she was going to marry him. Fliss hated it because he still used to go to her house to see them. He was like the son they never had."

"Would Felicity ever have got back with Rex, do you think?"

"It wouldn't have surprised me in the end. They were well suited. And he was very photogenic for her socials. And he used to take her to Wimbledon and Henley Regatta. And this new one wouldn't even be seen with her. She'd have soon got fed up with that."

"Where does Rex do the archery?"

"He goes all over the place. He's hoping to be at the next Olympics. I know Fliss used to go to the Becklesfield club and watch him. You don't think it's Rex, do you?"

"Seems funny she was killed by a bow and arrow. But it's a bit obvious."

"I wouldn't have thought he was the type. But you never know. I'm glad I've got my Marlon. We fell in love just before he signed with his first club. And he loves his family life. If he goes clubbing he always takes me."

"I'm so pleased for you. I can see nothing but happiness for you."

"Mind you, I miss living in London. It can feel very isolated here. Now my daughter has started school I can feel very alone."

Hayley looked to the left of Kylie. "Oh, you're not alone, hun. Did Heather tell you I'm a bit of a psychic? I don't know if you know, but there's a little girl standing next to you. She says she lives here."

Kylie looked and moved over a bit. "No, I didn't know. Who is she?"

"Her name is Gracie."

"A ghost?! But that's the name of Britney's imaginary friend. I've gone all shivery. She's had her since she was three, when we moved here a couple of years ago. I just thought it was because she's an only child. They always play with dolls together and have tea parties. It's Gracie this and Gracie that. Even, 'Gracie doesn't want to go to bed'. And I say, hard luck, Gracie. You're saying she's a ghost? Oh, my God, we'll have to move."

"She's a little girl. She won't hurt you," snapped Hayley. "She looks on you as her mummy. She's saying she doesn't know where her family is."

"That's sad, but so creepy. I don't think I want Britney playing with her anymore."

"Please don't say things like that. Spirits can be just as hurt as us. I know, believe me."

"How would you like to have a ghost there every day?"

Hayley looked over at Terry and Abigail. "I agree, it can be hard, but if she's been here for years, who can it hurt? And your daughter obviously enjoys her company. I'll see what I can do. For Gracie's sake, though. Perhaps we can find her own family and reunite them and then she can leave. Sweetie, have you got a second name? And when did you last see your mummy? Her second name is May and she doesn't know. Do you remember where you lived? In a big cottage with a red roof. Well, that might help, Gracie. I'm going to try and find Mummy and Daddy for you. Okay, and your brother, James. You stay here till then and we'll come back, I promise."

"But it's a new build. It can't be haunted."

"Anywhere can be haunted, hun. It could be the ground it's built on. I'm sure there used to be a house here called Edenbury Manor that they pulled down to build the estate. But in this case, a ghost has moved in."

"I'll have to get used to it, I suppose. God knows what Marlon will do," said Kylie. "It's quite sweet that she looks on me as her mummy. How old is she?"

"She's only six, bless her heart. Look, I've got to do some things for Felicity but I'll see what I can find out about Gracie. Can you remember how you died, sweetie? That means, er, when you came here and left your family. She can remember water. Well, we know the River Gore isn't far from here. She's in jeans and a top, so it's not fifty years ago or anything like that. It gives us somewhere to start." Hayley turned to Kylie. "Thank you so much for telling us about Felicity. And we'll come back as soon as we find out anything about Gracie. If you need anything, just call."

Kylie looked at the card.

The Deadly Detective Agency
All Problems Great & Small
Paranormal & Normal

Followed by an email address and a mobile number for Hayley Moon.

After she had let Hayley out she looked around and said, "Just you and me then, Gracie. Don't make me jump or anything, will you?" Kylie felt a fluttering in her hand that she had felt before, but had always thought it was an itch. She had even looked it up because she recalled it was some kind of superstition, and learnt an itchy palm meant you were going to lose money. Now she knew it was love. She decided not to say anything to her husband or daughter. It would take a lot of explaining to say that her new friend was actually dead. And Gracie was company for Britney, even if it was frightening. And Marlon would either put the house on the market or get all his friends round to contact the dead, neither of which she fancied.

Kylie suddenly thought that Hayley Moon had said, 'we will come back'. Who did she mean? Surely she was alone, or was it another ghost? She had felt suddenly cold as she invited her into the house. Kylie walked to the drinks cabinet and poured herself a neat gin.

"Don't judge, Gracie. Either you are here or I'm as crazy as that Moon lady!"

The crazy Moon lady had already started looking online for any articles about a young girl losing her life on the River Gore. Hayley went back ten years and there was nothing. There was plenty, however, about the murders they had solved at the Ottersmill Regatta. Not that their agency or even Hayley got mentioned. She would have to leave it for Tom to check their database at the police station for the death of Gracie May.

Tom wouldn't be able to for a while because he and Sergeant Mills were searching Felicity Fortescue's bedroom at her parents' house in Crockley-on-Edge. Oscar Fortescue had already threatened to report DCI Johnson to George Carson, the Chief Constable. Johnson assured him that he couldn't give a damn that they played golf together, and that he didn't appreciate him offering a reward as if the police weren't capable of finding the murderer. Johnson said all that would do is make sure that instead of getting a few calls with some real leads, they'd get inundated with useless information ringing on the off chance of getting twenty thousand pounds.

"So who are you? Her brother?" said Johnson to a blond-haired young man who had walked in the back door, sat down, and held the hand of Felicity's mother.

"Rex Dubois. I'm not related."

Mr Fortescue explained, "He's like our son. He used to be our daughter's boyfriend. We hoped they would marry, Inspector."

"Oh, yeah? And why didn't you, son?"

"Er, we were both busy doing our own thing. I've got my tennis and she had, well, you know. And I'm in training for the Olympic archery team."

Johnson gave a smile. "Are you? Now that is very interesting, seeing as I was just telling Mr and Mrs Fortescue that their lovely daughter may have been killed by an arrow."

"You're kidding me?" said Rex.

"I never kid, son. So you know how to shoot a bow, and you'd been dumped by the victim. That just leaves me to ask where you were on Friday the twenty-third at midday?"

Rex looked worried and looked at Mrs Fortescue for help. She was wondering if it could have been him as well, so she looked down into her lap.

"I'd never do that, you've got to believe me, Fiona. I was on my way back from Eastbourne. I'd been playing in a tournament. You can ask the hotel when I checked out. It was past nine o'clock and the traffic was awful. I didn't get back till gone one."

"Seems like a long time to me. What car do you drive, Mr Dubois?"

"Well, an Audi TT. But we still have to obey the speed limits."

"I'm sure, I'm sure. But it's not that good an alibi, is it?"

"I still loved Felicity."

"That's giving you more motive for murder. Unrequited love is up there with revenge and greed. I have no idea why myself," said Johnson.

"And she loved me. I couldn't tell you both, but we were thinking of getting back together. I didn't want to get your hopes up, Oscar."

Oscar Fortescue looked like he didn't believe him. His little girl would have told him.

DCI Johnson rubbed his hands together. The CC would be glad if they wrapped this one up quickly. With a bit of luck, his fancy car would be caught speeding heading for Ridgeway Wood.

"We'll be checking. And I don't think your name was mentioned lately on her Instagrams. I reckon she might have met someone else, giving you even more motive. So don't leave town, sir."

Johnson left Rex arguing his innocence to the suspicious parents and went to find Mills and Bennett.

Dave and the young PC were searching Felicity's room, which was as big as the bottom floor of Tom's house. Her wardrobe was the size of his bedroom. He was thankful that his wife didn't need all these clothes.

After twenty minutes they hadn't found much. Her parents thought she might have a new boyfriend, but they had no idea who it was and there was no sign of who it might be. Mrs Fortescue suggested her friend, Kylie Silver, might know. Dave didn't expect to find a diary in her room as her whole life was a live one for all her followers. And there was no sign of her missing phone that she would never have left home without. Her laptop had already been taken for analysis.

The only clue, 'Ridgeway Wood?', was written on the back of a receipt for a coffee shop in Gorebridge. She could have met her murderer there, thought Tom. Perhaps CCTV could show them who it was.

One thing was for sure: it was this person's idea to meet there, and they must have known about the bird hide. So it was even more important that Hayley went to the meeting of the BLB on Monday.

"Have you found anything, boys?" asked Johnson.

"Not much, sir. Only that she was going to meet someone at the wood," said Tom. "I'll get this receipt checked as well."

"Did you find anything about a bloke called Rex Dubois? He's her ex, and downstairs at the moment sucking up to the parents. He's as false as my granny's teeth."

Mills showed him a Valentine's card. "This was in the drawer. Says, 'You will be mine forever'. And look, there's a heart with an arrow going through it."

"'You will be mine forever' sounds a bit of a threat, I reckon. Bag it for evidence. And I haven't told you the best bit: he's into archery. If the Robin Hood cap fits and all that."

"I don't suppose he's into birds, is he, sir?" asked Tom.

"Of course he is. I just said he's Felicity's ex. What are you saying?"

"No, I meant like a birdwatcher. Because of where she was found."

"That's got nothing to do with anything, daft lad. The killer just came across that. Anyone could have known about it."

"I've lived in Becklesfield for years and I didn't know there were any, sir."

"Shows you're not very observant then. That's why I'm a DCI and you're a constable."

Tom hoped more than ever that Hayley would find the proof that it was something to do with the BLB. That would wipe that smile off his face and he could tell him where to stick...

"Bennett! Stop daydreaming. Go back to the station and find out all that you can about Rex Dubois."

Chapter 29

Tom had made sure he was back early from work to look after Benjie so Hayley could go to the meeting. He didn't even mind that Abigail and Terry were there. So, dead on seven o'clock, Hayley walked in the door of the Becklesfield Town Hall. Abigail reminded her not to mention that Felicity had been killed by an arrow. That had not been released to the public yet.

"Welcome to the BLB, Mrs Bennett," said Harold Harding. "I'm so pleased you decided to come."

"Hayley, please. There's quite a few here then."

"Usually we get a few more. Let me introduce you. Everyone, this is Hayley. She lives in the village and her little boy is interested in ornithology. This is Malcolm, our treasurer. Josephine, Linda, Brandon and Mick. Brandon, get Hayley a cup of tea."

"Thank you, no sugar."

"How is young Benjamin liking his parrot?"

"Oh, he loves it. Wants to take it to bed with him every night," lied Hayley. He much preferred the dinosaur.

"Have you got your bird table yet?"

"I've ordered one. You must tell me the best thing to feed

them. My mum used to throw stale bread out, but I'm guessing that's not right."

"Oh, my dear, things have changed. They know now that the mould can kill them and there are no nutrients in it. Seeds are good, and suet blocks. The garden centre has a good choice."

The tall lady with broad shoulders joined them. Hayley thought her name was Josephine. "Nuts."

"Sorry?" said Hayley.

"Peanuts, that's what I use. I put them in a feeder and hang them from the trees. Make sure you get one that's squirrel-proof. And water. People forget that. Birds have to drink as well."

"I had no idea there was so much to know," said Hayley.

"Shall we take a seat, ladies?" interrupted Harding.

A long table was set with paperwork and photos for each member. They must have been expecting more than the seven people that were there. Hayley thanked Brandon for her tea, but she wasn't sure that she fancied drinking it. He was a scruffy-looking boy with a definite case of body odour, greasy hair, and thick glasses. When Malcolm welcomed her again as he started the meeting, Hayley was starting to feel really guilty, but then she began to enjoy it. She even offered to help with the bird conservation ideas they had. And it was quite exciting to see all the photos of birds that she didn't even know existed, let alone that were so close to home.

"Were these all taken in Ridgeway Wood?" she asked Mick, a middle-aged man who was sitting next to her.

"These three were. That's a chiffchaff. I took that one and Malcolm took the other two. These are from the lavender meadow, and Linda took this one of the common greenshank on the east coast last week."

"They're beautiful photos. I suppose I'd need a better camera than the one on my phone."

"To get the quality, yes. But we all have to start somewhere," said Mick.

"I'm starting to get bored," said Abigail to Terry. "I can't think of anything worse than being a member of this… Although, on the other hand, it could be just what I need to do on a Monday night. Don't you agree, Hayley?"

Hayley frowned and was surprised to hear Abigail say that until she looked over towards the open door. She coughed the word, "Yes," behind her hand.

Terry was puzzled as well until he saw the reason for Abigail's sudden change of heart. The reason was about six feet tall, well-built and handsome, possibly ex-military.

"I'll be his bird any day," said Abigail.

"Oh, now you don't mind being a bird. Can't see he's anything special myself."

"But I'm wondering if Felicity did. He's the only likely one here, isn't he? Whoever he is could be the murderer, actually. She said he was gorgeous, so that rules anyone else out here. Mind you, could it be a jealous wife? I wonder if he's married. She could have meant Josephine's or Linda's husbands. Josephine looks strong enough. Something else to check."

The new arrival made straight for Hayley. "Hello, I see the membership is taking a turn for the better. Alex Anderson."

"Hayley Bennett. Are you a regular member?" Hayley asked hopefully.

"I wouldn't say regular, no."

"Nor would I," said Mr Harding sulkily. "He hasn't been for months." Hayley would say that the male members were quite pleased about that.

Alex looked at the photographs on the table and told Hayley, "I'm more into birds of prey."

Terry mumbled, "I reckon he preys on birds."

Hayley answered, "That's very interesting. Are there many round here?"

"There's the obvious ones, like the red kite. Their numbers have soared, much like the birds," he added as he smiled, which made him even more popular with the two ladies. "But favourites of mine are peregrine falcons, goshawks and kestrels. Have a look, I took these recently." He bent close to her and swiped through the photographs on his phone.

"Amazing photos, Alex. Is that a chiffchaff? I just saw one of those."

"Well, if I see something I snap it. But this is the best one—the golden eagle."

"Beautiful. But not in England, surely?"

"No, not here. I travel all over," said Alex boastfully.

Mick, sitting on the other side of Hayley, tried to get her attention once more. "I prefer to keep local. You can't beat your own back garden. Hayley's son is very interested," he added deliberately.

"She doesn't look old enough to have a son," he replied. It obviously didn't put him off.

Terry said, "He's a bit smarmy, isn't he?"

"It's called being a gentleman. I rather like him. Except he's stopping Hayley from concentrating. Why isn't Hayley grilling them about the murder?"

"They're still on about birds. She'll have to wait till after the meeting maybe. And you have to blend in first. It would look suspicious otherwise. And she's learned that at least two of them have been to Ridgeway in the last month: Mick and Malcolm. Either of them could have carried Felicity and known where to put the body," said Terry.

"Tom checked the receipt at the coffee shop and she was there with her mum, so she must have just taken it out of her bag to write on. It could be anyone that came up to her. We haven't got any more clues to go on," said Abigail.

"I've just thought of something weird," said Terry. "I'm

going to sound like Betty, but what's that saying or rhyme about Cock Robin?"

"If Betty was here, I dread to think what she would say to that."

"No, I'm serious, Abs."

"Then I have no idea. Cock Robin?"

"It's on the tip of my tongue. Um, I know," Terry said with relief. "It goes: 'Who killed Cock Robin? I, said the sparrow, with my bow and arrow.'"

"So we're looking for a homicidal sparrow. That's not exactly helpful."

"I know, but I used to like it. I'll get Suzie to look it up in the library."

"So does he get arrested?" asked Abigail.

"Who?"

"The sparrow. He obviously confessed."

"I don't think he does. The other animals just talk about burying him," said Terry. "Accessories after the fact, I suppose."

"Our murderer is going to get away with it too if Hayley doesn't stop going on about birds."

Hayley, who had been listening to Malcolm as well as the two ghosts, said a bit too loudly, "Did you hear about the poor girl they found in one of your bird cabins? I don't suppose any of you saw anything when you were in Ridgeway, did you?"

"I haven't been there for over a month. It's terrifying," said Linda. "I won't be going there on my own until they've caught whoever did it."

"It was the hide at the far edge I heard," said Mick. "I didn't think anyone used that one anymore. Too far to walk from the car park."

"Probably why it was chosen," said Brandon.

Harding added, "I heard she wasn't from around here, so what was she doing there?"

"I wish I was there," said Brandon wistfully. "Did you hear

about the reward? Twenty thousand. What I could do with that."

"I know," said Mick. "Someone will get it. A dog walker or something. That poor dad though. Your heart breaks for him."

"And the mother," said Josephine. "I wonder if she was, you know. And they haven't said how she was killed yet."

"I'm surprised the poor girl's body was found at all," said Alex Anderson, to which Abigail said, "Perhaps that's why he's here, to find out how she was found so quickly after he killed her."

"Yes, I wonder how the murderer knew it was there. It's mainly for birdwatchers, isn't it?" said Hayley, which made them all turn to stare at her.

"Hayley's husband is our village bobby," said Harold Harding.

That shut them all up, and no one admitted to being in the woods at the time or having ever been where the body had been found. Then Malcolm said it was time to end the meeting.

Mr Harding told her, "We only get the hall for an hour, then it's the ladies and their Patchwork Parlez meeting."

"Would you like me to help put the table and chairs away?" Hayley offered.

"No, thank you. Brandon will do that. Brandon, get a move on, the ladies will be here in a minute."

"Can I take the pictures home?"

"Please do, Hayley. And we hope to see you next month. I've got the perfect book I'd like to give you for Benjamin. It's got all the British birds in."

"That's so nice of you. I'll definitely come next time if Tom is back home in time to babysit. Do you live locally, Alex?"

"Upper Goreton, so not far."

"So do you do photography for a living?" asked Hayley.

"No. Actually, I'm a private detective."

Abigail was in shock. "What? A private detective? Who does he think he is?"

"Not so great now then," said Terry. "He is allowed to be, you know. Bet he's a good one going by his clothes." He was enjoying this.

"Rubbish. How come we've never heard of him? Tom has never mentioned him. It all makes sense now. He's no more interested in birds than the man on the moon. He's after the reward, I bet. Well, he's not going to solve the murder before us, Terry."

"You thought he might be the murderer earlier," said Terry, "and just here to do a bit of fishing."

"I hope he is. But if not, I'm not letting him get any help from Hayley. Did you hear that? He just asked Hayley if she wanted to go for a drink with him? Of all the nerve. He knows she's married to a policeman. He probably wants to find out what they know."

But Hayley had no intention of going. "Sorry, no. I have to get back to my husband. Are you on the case? Or do you know anything about the girl that was murdered?"

Alex rubbed his nose and gave a small shrug of his left shoulder. "No, nothing at all. Pure coincidence that I chose to come tonight." Hayley didn't have to be a psychic to know he was lying. "I'd better get going then. Hopefully I'll see you around, Hayley."

"I expect you will," she answered. "Bye, Alex."

"He'll see me around," said Abigail angrily. "What a cheek, Hayley. Shonking in on our investigation."

"We'll talk outside," she whispered.

Terry had a good idea. "I'll go with him and see where he lives and what he does. Give the PI a taste of his own medicine."

"Brilliant idea. Gives a whole new meaning to the words 'shadowing someone'," said Abigail. "We'll see you at the library later."

The Deadly Coaching Inn

Terry followed him to an old estate car. It didn't go with his clothes or demeanour, but Terry guessed it was perfect for stakeouts or long surveillances. He thought Alex must do a lot, because it was the messiest and most disgusting car he had ever been in. He was glad he couldn't smell anymore. The floor and the passenger seat were covered in food wrappers and half-finished drinks. On the back seat was a bottle that he was hoping contained apple juice, but he had a feeling it wasn't.

So Terry was expecting the flat he followed him into would be the same, but it was much tidier. Alex opened a can of beer out of the fridge and sat at his dining room table. Terry guessed this was the sole office of the Alex Anderson Detective Agency. There were no signs of a wife who could be a suspect.

Alex picked up a recorder and talked into it.

"Monday, 8.35 pm. Report for my client—This evening I attended the monthly meeting of the birdwatchers' club in Becklesfield. Present were Harold, Mick, Brandon, Malcolm, Linda, Josephine and a lady who I didn't know—Hayley Bennett. She is married to the local policeman which made it very suspicious. I don't believe she is interested in the subject. Was she there to find out information for the police or for the reward? Or a more sinister reason? Did Felicity know her or her husband? None of the other members seem to know much about the murder. It was Hayley who brought up the subject. Brandon mentioned the reward. Tomorrow I shall be investigating another angle—Rex Dubois and his connection to archery. Were any of the people tonight capable of firing a bow with such precision into the back of a moving target?"

Terry was wondering how he knew so much about the cause of death.

"We have Harold—shopkeeper. Malcolm—prison guard. Brandon—salesman. Mick—gardener. Linda—housewife. Josephine—office clerk. Hayley—I have no idea. She has a child so perhaps she doesn't work. But she was a strange woman. She looked like a hippy witch with her straight black hair and long skirt and beads. I even saw her talking to herself at one point. Unless she was wired and was talking to her husband. Wired or weird, I'll have to find out. Or recording everyone to get the reward. Could she have killed Felicity because of jealousy? How is she connected? Either way, she would have been burned at the stake at one time.

"So also in the morning I'll be paying a visit to the photographer, Philip Gowdy. It's funny he took a photo but didn't see anything. Then I'll be following Rex Dubois and talking to some of his friends to see if he was obsessed with the deceased or if he was really getting back with her. Has he got an alibi? And I will see her three friends whose names I've been given. I'll put some feelers out to find out more about Hayley of Becklesfield. I have my suspicions about her. Not just because she's weird and witchy."

The weird and witchy lady herself left the club after a quick goodbye to the rest of the members. She was in no hurry to get back. Usually she had to rush back for her mother-in-law to get off home, but Tom was his dad. So she walked slowly and stopped when she got to the bench overlooking the village pond.

"So what do we think of the private eye?" asked Hayley.

"I thought he was great until he dared to say he was a detective. I thought we were the only PIs in the village."

"Actually, I know how you feel. I was surprised. It felt strange. It's usually me asking questions with an ulterior motive, and then he was doing it. I'm not sure who was grilling who."

Abigail looked thoughtful. "He did say something suspicious, but I can't remember what it was now. I wonder if he's any good."

"I'll look on my phone. He must have a website. Upper Goreton, that's him. 'AA Private Investigations. Professional and confidential work undertaken. Surveillance, background checks and missing persons found. Let us gather evidence for you using the latest technology. Phone or email for a private appointment. Affordable rates.'"

"He might have the latest technology, but he hasn't got a Hayley Moon," said Abigail.

"Or your brilliant brain, hun. So is Alex after the reward, or does he want to see if anyone knows he was seeing Felicity? If he is good, he might know who I am. He might have been following me and wanted to strike up a conversation at the club."

"I don't trust him," said Abigail. "Terry's right, he is smarmy. He'll know his address by now, so we'll pay Alex a visit tomorrow. He's missing a Suzie as well. We can do a search and a surveillance and be in the same room."

"Good idea, hun."

"Chiffchaff!"

"Bless you," joked Hayley.

"No. I've just thought, Alex showed you a photo he'd taken of a chiffchaff. And someone else had and said it was from Ridgeway Wood. So that might prove he was there recently. Good job you went tonight, because we got plenty of information, didn't we?"

"Actually, I was rather enjoying that meeting. It was better than I thought it would be," said Hayley. "They're really nice people and it was interesting."

"I'd rather have gone to Patchwork Parlez," said Abigail.

"Not with my sewing skills, hun. At least they're doing something for the birds. Did you know that the bird population has decreased by sixteen percent since the seventies?"

"So might more women if we don't find the killer."

"Fair point, hun. I didn't talk to anyone who came across as guilty. Not that I can always tell. If they don't feel guilty then I don't sense it. Apart from Alex and Brandon, Mick and Malcolm look too old for Felicity, but who knows."

"Brandon's too nerdy," said Abigail. "And he was sweaty and had greasy hair and dirty nails. Josephine and Linda are no great shakes either, but their husbands might be. That is, if they're married."

"They are, I looked for rings," said Hayley. "Linda was very keen to let everybody know that she'd been away when she took her photos last week. And Josephine apologised for not taking any as she'd been too busy at work to have time."

"Methinks the ladies doth protest too much," said Abigail. "There I go again. I swear we're all turning into Betty. Terry's as bad. Hayley, have you heard about a sparrow who killed a robin?"

"To be honest, hun, I've had quite enough of birds for a while. What with the three crows, the ones tonight and the parrot. And did I tell you that Johnson has got a bee in his bonnet about Rex Dubois, who hasn't got an alibi yet? Oh, God, now we've got the birds and the bees. Talking of which, I'd better go back and kiss Benjie night-night. Tom was going to bath him and put him to bed, thank goodness. It's nice to have a night off."

But when Hayley got home, she didn't know whether to shout or get her phone out and take a picture. Benjie was fast asleep as she had hoped. In fact, they all were. Trouble was, he was on the sitting room floor, with Luna's head resting on his tummy, and next to him was his snoring father. So she took another photo to add to the thousand others.

And it was lucky for Tom that he did get some extra sleep, because his phone rang before seven o'clock the next morning. A dog on his early morning walk had run off and started to dig something up. The owner, a pensioner from Becklesfield, had gone to look and then taken out his phone to ring for help. There was another girl's body in Ridgeway Wood.

Chapter 30

LILLIAN AND ABIGAIL MADE FOR RIDGEWAY WOOD AS soon as they heard about the girl. A white tent had been erected over the body and the yellow tape, blowing in the wind, was holding the locals back from contaminating the crime scene.

Abigail noticed a man with his dog talking to Tom, and she guessed the Golden Retriever on the lead was the one who had found the body. His owner, Paul Bradford, was thinking that if he'd known how long he was going to be kept there, he would have kept walking. She also noticed the private detective, Alex Anderson, was as near the crime scene as he could get. He was recording everything on his phone, and she wished Suzie was there to knock it out of his hand. Surely he couldn't be as good as them. She would just die if he got to the murderer before her. Abigail wondered how he had heard about the murder so quickly. He didn't even live in the area. Alex was even nearer the top of her list of the guilty.

Inside the tent, examining the body, was Dr Malik. She had just been joined by DCI Johnson, who had just arrived.

"It's a sad day, Tony."

"You're right there, Doctor. This poor lass looks even

younger. I swear to God I'll make whoever did this pay. Have we got an ID yet?"

"One of the locals said her name is Molly Travis of Becklesfield. I think by now her parents might have heard. I hope not."

"Mills, get there quick. No one deserves to hear that through the village gossips."

"Will do, sir. We did get a call from a Mrs Travis late last night to say her daughter hadn't come home. But it was too early to call her a missing person. Damn shame."

Abigail made a decision to go with Mills. "Lillian, you stay here and listen to what the doctor says. You'll understand more than me. I'll meet you back at Hayley's."

Johnson asked the doctor, "Is it connected to the Fortescue lass?"

"Too early to say. But look at this. The attack was from the front, but the puncture wound looks just the same as the one made by the arrow. But this time it went straight through to the heart and death was immediate."

"So whoever did it could have been an Olympic archer. I've got one in mind."

"I won't know for sure till I do the autopsy, but if this was made by an arrow, I don't think it was fired. It hasn't gone deep enough. I think this may have been pushed in by hand. Someone was trying to make it look like the same MO. I have no idea why. But that's up to you to find out."

"So two killers?"

"Not necessarily, Tony, but maybe. I'll be able to tell you if the tip is the same, probably later today."

"When do you think she was killed?"

"Last evening, between five and eight. I can't be more accurate yet. Have you got a suspect then?"

"Let's just say I've got one young lad in my sights. Be interesting to know where he was yesterday. Okay, thank you, Dr

Malik. You can take the body now, boys. But be very gentle with her."

Lillian saw a different side to Johnson for the first time. There was even a tear in his eye. He cared about these girls. He wanted to get justice for these girls. There was hope for humanity, she thought.

Mills cared too. He almost hoped that he didn't have to be the one to tell Molly's family. As he got closer, he could see that he wouldn't have to. The front door of the small house was open and one neighbour was going in and two were coming out. Mills tapped on the glass and went in, followed by Abigail.

A younger lady was kneeling before a middle-aged woman and holding both of her hands. The one he presumed was Molly's mother was in shock and was wishing everyone would go. She wanted to scream or cry, she wasn't sure which. Either way, if it was true, she didn't want to go on. And now a man was here. Police? More than likely. He said his name was Sergeant Mills and he had a kind face. Thankfully, he told everyone to go.

"I'm so sorry for your loss, Mrs Travis. Is there anyone I can call for you?"

"My sister is on her way from London. My husband passed away last year. I've only got my Molly." She sniffed and looked away.

"I hate to have to ask you a few things, but do you know what she was doing at Ridgeway Wood yesterday?"

"I didn't kiss her. Yesterday morning when she left for work. I didn't kiss her goodbye. She always used to come over and kiss me and say 'see you tonight, Mum'. But she was late for work, you see. She never was very good at getting out of bed. Now I'll never get another kiss."

Mills didn't know what to say, so he waited until she was

ready to carry on. He looked around the room at the photographs of a fair-haired toddler, the same girl in her school uniform, and culminating in one of her in a puffy-sleeved bridesmaid's dress. Molly was smiling, not knowing that she would never be a bride herself. What would he do if he lost his treasured daughter?

"Sorry, Sergeant. I don't know what she was doing in the woods. She knew I didn't like her going there on her own. But she did say she might be late home, so I wasn't worried to start with. When it got to eleven I knew there was something wrong."

"Where did she work?"

"In the shop at the garage just outside the village. She'd walk there and back. I don't drive. I can, but I don't. I sold the car when Frank died."

"Could it have been one of her friends she was meeting?"

"It must have been someone. Molly was a quiet girl and didn't go out much. She had her school friends, and she'd never been the sort to go clubbing like some. There was no boyfriend that I knew of."

"Was she in good spirits when she left?"

"Very. Almost excited about something. I had a go at her about being late and she said it wouldn't matter soon. I don't know what she meant and she didn't say."

"Did Molly often go to the woods?"

"Only if we took the dog. That's Teddy, he's in the garden. She did take him a week or so ago."

Abigail and Mills were thinking the same thing. Molly was hoping to meet someone there to talk about the reward. Or maybe blackmailing the killer to get more if she had seen something. Whatever happened, she got more than she bargained for.

"Do you know which day it was?"

"She has Fridays and Saturdays off from the shop, so it must have been then. Friday, I think. But she didn't have Teddy with her after work yesterday, so why was she there?"

"We'll find out, Mrs Travis. Did she know a girl called Felicity Fortescue?"

"So it's something to do with that. I thought it must be. No, we chatted about the murder and she didn't know her. But she wouldn't. Going by the family, they wouldn't have known us. So you think it's some type of maniac killing young girls, do you?"

"We don't know much of anything yet. But we will, I promise you."

"There's one thing I have to know, Sergeant. Did she suffer?"

Mills thought back to the small face and the fair hair spread out above her head; her long eyelashes resting on the pale cheeks. He tried to forget the rest of her slight body, blemished by the soil and leaves. "No, I'm sure Molly didn't suffer. She passed very quickly."

"Good, good," her mother whispered quietly. "How can I go on living without her, Sergeant?"

"I'm so sorry." Dave moved next to her and held her tightly. Not as a policeman, but as a parent, and they both cried.

Chapter 31

"We think of the police as hard, but they're human too," said Abigail.

"You don't have to tell me that, hun. Tom has cried many a time about what he's seen. And Dave is a gentle soul as well."

"It even got to Johnson," said Lillian. "She looked so innocent and pure lying there."

"When Dave held her, it was one of the most tender moments that I've ever seen. Molly's mum will never be the same again. Her whole world has gone. Apart from her dog."

"I feel so sorry for her," said Betty. "I wish I could go round there and help her."

"So let's get justice as soon as we can," said Hayley. "We don't want another girl to be found."

"At least Molly died quicker than Felicity. So Dr Malik thinks. An arrow to the heart, and not in the good way," said Lillian.

"Perhaps that's what this is about; Cupid's bow," said Abigail. "He thinks he's Cupid. Or is it Eros?"

"Cupid is Roman and Eros is Greek, I think," said Lillian. "The arrow was supposed to make them fall in love. I think you might be right. When he couldn't get Felicity or Molly to fall in love with him, he killed them."

"And Molly went willingly and said she was going to be late, so she must have known whoever it was. And she didn't think she would be in danger, so I don't think it's blackmail. As far as we know, she was single, so she could have been going on a first date and it went wrong. Even a blind date. Girls are so trusting at that age. She could have met him online. We might have to rethink everything."

"I agree, Abi. You said her mum said she was excited to go, not worried," added Hayley.

"But she went straight from work. Surely if it was a date she would have gone home to get changed first. I would have done," said Abigail. "We know the PI Alex Anderson was in the area last night. He needs looking at as well. So we can't rule out that she thought or knew they were there when Felicity was killed and they could share the reward. And perhaps this person didn't want to share."

"So not the murderer of Felicity, but another witness. If Molly told her mum in the morning that she was going to be late, she must have contacted that person the night before," added Lillian.

Betty said, "So they had plenty of time to get something that resembled an arrow, if you get the geese."

"Geese, Betty?" said Hayley. "I swear to God, we don't need any more birds. But I do get the gist, hun. You mean like a sharpened bit of bamboo or something."

"Exactly. But that makes it even worse because we're looking for two different murderers then. It's hard enough to find one. Perhaps it was Rex Dubois. This new killer would get more in blackmail than the reward. He could keep going back for more. Rex sounds like he's got plenty of money."

"By the law of averages, Johnson should be right once in a while. What else did Mrs Travis say?" asked Lillian.

Abigail repeated everything. She was finding it hard to concentrate as Benjie was starting to grizzle in his high chair. Luna took the opportunity to start meowing to let them know that he was ready for some attention as well. At the very least, lunch. Benjie went one step further and threw his toy car across the room.

"Won't be long, sweetie," Hayley assured him. But Benjie knew what she was like when she got talking to the others, and started with the crocodile tears and the wailing.

"Give him that parrot," said Lillian.

"I'll try, but he doesn't like it very much. It's supposed to repeat what you say, but it's broken." Hayley put it in front of him, but he cried even more. So she took it off him and put it on the kitchen worktop.

Lillian tried to reason with him. "Don't cry, Benjamin. Mummy's very busy. She'll get you out in a minute." She had worked in the children's ward when she was alive, so she was good with children. But the young boy was not in a mood to be pacified, and the crying got louder.

Hayley felt it going through her head like a knife through butter.

"Benjamin Bennett, will you shut up for five minutes!"

That shut them all up, even Luna.

"That's not like you, Hayl," said Abigail.

"Sometimes you just have to. Come on, sweetheart. Mummy will get you something to eat."

Luna was feeling left out and would rather that it was him getting something to eat. He jumped up and sat next to the parrot thing that was on the side. Three gentle taps with his curved paw and it fell to the ground. It did not get him the response he had hoped for.

"Luna, what have you done now! I was going to take it back to the shop tomorrow. Someone might like it."

Hayley dusted it off and pressed the button. It suddenly worked and the wings started flapping.

They all listened in shock as it repeated the last thing that had been spoken into it.

The parrot squawked, "By this time next week, hopefully he'll be dead."

"Did I just hear right?" said Abigail.

"You did, hun."

"You did, hun," said the high-pitched reply from the parrot.

"Whoever owned it last must have said that. Mrs Malloy said a lady brought it in the day before I bought it. With some men's clothes, which doesn't bode well. It had been her nephew's. And that was about a week ago, which is rather worrying."

The parrot tried to keep up with Hayley but just emitted a high-pitched noise while flapping excitedly.

"Trouble is, it's gone now. It might be on a tape inside though. Try turning it off and on again," suggested Abigail.

Turning it on again didn't get the voice back. "But it could be anyone. A man or a woman."

The parrot started repeating Hayley again. "A man or a woman."

"Turn it off," said Lillian. "What an awful noise."

"I think it was a woman," said Hayley. "Just a feeling I have. I wonder if we're too late."

Lillian said, "I haven't heard of any men being murdered. But it might not be round here. And it might even be a natural death. Perhaps he's been ill and in pain and his wife hopes he'll be out of his misery."

"I'm not so sure, hun. You know I think I've been given this ability for a reason, so we can't just forget about it. I'll pop and see Mrs Malloy when I get time. But you might well be right, Lillian."

"I think we need to concentrate on these murders first, just in case Robin is planning another one. That's Robin Hood, not Cock Robin," said Abigail.

"Who's Cock Robin?" said Lillian.

"You'll have to ask Terry. I have no idea. But I think he might be dead. Don't ask, Lillian."

"I love that poem. We had to learn it at school. I'm surprised you don't know *Who Killed Cock Robin*, Abigail."

"I'm sure I'd have got there in the end, Betty. Especially if there was a witness."

"There was. The fly saw him die."

"I think we're getting a bit off topic, hun. And I'm so sorry I shouted, sweetie," Hayley said, picking up Benjie and kissing his cheek.

Lillian said, "You're his mummy. He knows you don't mean it."

"I know, but I don't like to. And he is a good little boy most of the time. I'll feed you right now. Yes, and you too, Luna."

Abigail looked thoughtful. "Hmm, that would explain that at least. But not the rest of it."

Lillian looked at Hayley and said to Abigail, "Are you having one of your brainwaves?"

"A small nipple—I mean ripple," she answered, looking at Benjie having his bottle of milk. "I need to have a proper think now it's quiet."

Abigail sat back in her chair and talked to herself. "So they know each other. But would she do that? And Damien Shadow is proof of that. We need to ask first."

"Damien Shadow, hun? Is it all connected to The Three Crows?"

"Not exactly. It's just a little idea I've got."

"Can I help, hun?"

"Er, is the charity shop open? Or is it closed for lunch?" asked Abigail.

Hayley looked at her watch. "It's open. But I'm not sure if Mrs Malloy is there today."

"It's not Mrs Malloy we need to talk to. I'll explain on the way."

Hayley pushed open the door to Wet & Wildlife and was pleased to see Mr Harding hanging up men's shirts in the far corner.

"Hello, Hayley. I've got that book I told you about." He went behind the counter. "Here it is — *Birds of the British Isles*."

"That's so kind of you. You'll treasure it all your life, won't you, Benjie? Do I owe you anything?"

"Of course not. It was my son's. But he never looks at it any more. As I said, make the most of it. They grow up so fast."

"Well, thank you. I actually wanted to ask you if you knew where we could find Brandon? I met him at the meeting and wanted to ask him something."

Mr Harding looked up at the clock. "He'll be at work. If it's about insurance, he'll be there till about five. It's on the high street in Chortle. It's only about twenty minutes' walk down the bridle path. Mind you, he sometimes goes home for lunch."

"I don't suppose you have his home address then, do you?"

Mr Harding smiled. "I thought you knew, Hayley. He lives at home with me. He's my son."

Hayley looked back at Abigail and said, "No. I did not know that. Thank you for the book. I'll see you soon."

Hayley had a bit of trouble getting the pushchair out of the narrow door, mainly because she was a bit annoyed at Abigail.

"Did you know Brandon was his son?"

"Not for sure, I promise. I needed to check first. But now I know, let's go and see him. There's something else I have to find out."

"I can't think what," said Hayley. "Unless he was the other person that was after the reward."

"You're getting warmer," said Abigail.

"And he killed Molly to get all the reward."

"Cold again, Hayl."

"But he didn't kill Felicity. There's no way, even with the real Cupid's arrow, that he could get someone like Felicity Fortescue. I'm surprised he's got a job selling insurance. I thought he was a car mechanic, going by his dirty nails."

Abigail stopped walking and said, "Of course they were dirty. He'd just buried Molly."

Lillian and Hayley stopped too.

"Mr Harding's son?" said Hayley. "I can't believe it. I know he said he was having trouble with him, but that's going a bit far. How did you work out he was his son in the first place?"

"That was thanks to you this morning. When you lost it with Benjie, it made me think that family can get annoyed with each other and we never treat our family so politely as we do friends. It's natural. Remember Mr Harding at the meeting? It was, 'Brandon, make the tea. Brandon, put the chairs away'. So it was just a hunch. Then, like you say, we know he'd changed from when he was a nice young boy. But we'll soon find out. At least we've solved part of it before that private detective. Terry said he hadn't got a clue. Apart from being suspicious of you."

"I heard weird and witchy, I think he said."

"He's kinda right," said Abigail sweetly.

They reached the high street in Chortle, and by then Benjie was fast asleep.

Hayley told the others that she wouldn't be taking him in the insurance shop until she was sure that Brandon didn't have anything to do with the murder of Molly.

They looked through the window and were disappointed not to see him inside. There was a girl with a client to the left, and there was a handsome man who was showing another to his desk.

"That's not him, is it?" said Lillian. "You never said he looked like that."

"No. Yes. No. It can't be, can it, Abigail?"

This Brandon was in a shirt and tie with his hair brushed back and no glasses. And most remarkable was the smile that lit up his face.

"It is, you know," said Hayley. "I'm beginning to see what Felicity saw in him. He looked so different at the meeting."

Abigail nodded. "As I said, it's like Damien Shadow."

"I see what you mean now, hun. But back the other way. You can never tell how someone looks for sure. I guess we all have good days and bad days. And I expect he would have looked sweaty if he had had to run all the way back from Ridgeway Wood to get an alibi at the BLB. And we haven't got an ounce of proof. But sorry, hun, I'm not sure he killed Felicity or even knew her."

Something caught Brandon's eye that made him lose his thread with his client. Was that the Hayley woman from the meeting? The weird woman was talking to herself. But then he recalled that his dad had said she was married to a policeman. Perhaps she was wired with a microphone and going to come and talk to him. Else why was she spying on him? Brandon started thinking she might have been on to him at the meeting. Damn, he should have washed his hands better. Had she taken the cup that he had made her tea in? Probably gave it to her husband for fingerprints. Could they get fingerprints off clothes? He excused himself from the customer and went outside. She had gone but he could see her pushing a child and going towards Becklesfield. It was okay though, he knew where she lived.

Chapter 32

As soon as the other spirits of the DDA had been told, they met back at Hayley's house. She had rung Tom and asked him to check if Brandon Harding had a criminal record of any kind and was waiting to hear back.

Terry still couldn't believe it was that weedy-looking man at the BLB.

"I think you're wrong this time, love. There's nothing to connect Brandon with Molly."

"Molly's mum said that she didn't go out clubbing or anything and the only friends she had were the ones from school. There's nothing on her phone, so she didn't get in touch any other way. But they both live in the village and she would only have had to ask him to meet. She could have popped into the insurance shop or seen him on her way to work. And I'm betting they were both about nineteen and in the same year. We can soon check. I'm only guessing, but I reckon she saw him there the day she took the dog. I bet she saw Felicity and wanted to check that was the day. Molly might have seen him on the other side of the wood and presumed he didn't have any information about the girl's death. And I think she would have seen if he was carrying a weapon, so she wasn't worried. Just wanted to see if he knew anything that could help her get the reward. I'm guessing it was the most exciting thing that had ever happened to her. She might get the money and even a bit of fame. After all, the victim was a huge social media influencer, I think they call them."

"Johnson thinks it's Rex Dubois. I think he might be right this time," said Terry. "Both killed by an arrow."

"But Rex wouldn't have needed to push the arrow in. He wouldn't have missed. Anyway, how would a girl who very rarely went out of Becklesfield know how to get hold of him?"

"Okay, so Brandon met her and he'd also heard about the reward. But he wanted to make it look like the other killer had done it. So he either gets an arrow from somewhere or he improvises. A sharpened stick might work just as well. So you're saying they met after they had both finished work, he killed Molly and then had to race back to the town hall, hence being hot and sweaty?"

"Correct, Terry. Although, a sharpened stick in a wood of sticks is going to be hard to find."

Suzie said, "But who killed Felicity? And who hired that private detective?"

"There's only one reason that anyone would have chosen an arrow," said Abigail. "One, because they're good at it."

"Told you," said Terry.

She gave him a look. "Two, because they want it to look like they were good at it. Kill two birds with one arrow, as you would say, Betty. So it could have been Brandon trying to frame Rex. Rex said he and Felicity might get back together and I believe him. She'd no doubt enjoyed her time with Brandon, he was something different. But Kylie said she would soon get fed up with not attending the likes of Wimbledon with a man on her arm. And Terry, Brandon was good-looking. It's surprising what smart clothes, styled hair and contact lenses can do."

"I can ask Tom, but he needs to get some proof before they can take him in for questioning. And they can't just go into his house and do a search, hun."

"No, but we can," said Suzie.

Apart from Hayley, they all decided to go to Brandon Harding's house. Mr Harding was in the shop and Brandon himself was at work until five. This was one of the few times that Hayley wished she was a ghost too. She had to stay at home with Benjie.

The Hardings had one of the small houses in Windmill Lane.

"Is there a Mrs Harding?" Abigail asked Terry. "I've never heard him mention her."

"I think they got divorced about five years ago. I did hear that the children had taken it hard. I don't think Harold minded much."

"So the house will be empty. Not that it matters. Lillian and Betty, can you look downstairs? Me, Terry and Suzie can look in his room. There's got to be something there. Perhaps something of Felicity's, or even the bow. Suzie will find it."

Brandon had the smallest bedroom that overlooked the street.

"Well, it's as messy as he was when we first saw him," said Abigail as they walked in. "That's another thing, he would never have been able to take Felicity home to meet the family. He probably didn't even tell her where he lived. Maybe even what he did for a living. I feel a bit sorry for him actually. It was probably love for him; a bit of rough for her. So, Terry, imagine you had a secret girlfriend, or any girlfriend, where would you put the evidence?"

"You mean all my love letters from adoring girls?"

"Well, I was thinking of something believable, but if you must."

"Er, a shoebox under the bed? It would have to be something large to take them all."

"Do people have shoeboxes these days? Okay, Suzie, have a look."

"There's a few dirty socks. Oh, my God, a plate of something that used to be food. Just a mouldy lump now. Nothing here."

"Try the drawer next to the bed, Suzie."

That was not much tidier either. Suzie took the papers out and spread them on top. Terry said it was normal things for a bloke: like three reels of electrical tape, screwdrivers, free samples of toothpaste, half a roll of toilet paper and old receipts. There were two things that got Abigail's attention.

"A ticket to get in Lord's cricket ground from one month ago and a leaflet from a trip up the Thames. Not a smoking arrow, but neither of those are cheap. And look, Suzie, open that. That means something, doesn't it?"

"You're right, Abigail. It's an application for a new passport that he signed two weeks ago but never sent."

"I wonder why. Not proof he's a double murderer though," said Terry. "Try the wardrobe. If the bow's not under the bed it has to be in there."

But Lillian shouted up the stairs, "Come here quick." Terry, Abigail and Suzie went downstairs thinking they had found something. So they were surprised to see Brandon was in the hall and going up the stairs two at a time.

"What's he doing home?" said Abigail. "That can't be good. Perhaps he's going to do a runner. Tom might have found something on his record and he heard about it. Let's see what he does. Oh, that's not good. That's bad, that's very bad."

Brandon Harding had pulled out a box from behind his clothes in the wardrobe. Inside was a black bag. He opened it, took something out, and put it inside his jacket. It was done deftly, even though he had no idea he was being watched. But there was no doubt what it was—a twenty-eight-inch arrow, with red feathers and a stainless-steel tip. Brandon ran down the stairs and slammed the front door behind him.

"I don't know where he's going, but it's not good," said Abigail. "Come on, we can't lose him. It wouldn't be Molly's mother, would it?"

"Could be," said Lillian. "He might think she'd told her something. I hope not."

None of them could believe it when he got on a bike that was hidden down the side of the house.

They were running, but Brandon was getting further away. He turned right out of Windmill Lane, which led to the high street. The spirits all shouted the same thing as they realised he was heading for Church Lane.

"Hayley!"

Chapter 33

HAYLEY HAD PUT BENJIE IN HIS COT AND WAS PUTTING the washing away in his cupboard. She was singing a lullaby, hoping he might have a nap so she could get the next lot of laundry done. She could never work out why she had to do so much for one so small.

As Hayley was putting his socks in the top drawer, she stopped stone dead. Benjie looked at her too, sensing something was wrong. Someone dangerous was approaching, and she suddenly knew who it was.

She closed the drawer silently and thought she heard the back door opening slowly and carefully. She had taken the washing off the line earlier and, living in a village, never thought that she would need to lock it.

Hayley put her finger to her lips in case Benjie cried out. Her phone was in the kitchen, so she was going to have to fight for their lives. Or should she pick Benjie up and try to get to the front door? She looked through the window overlooking the back garden and knew they would never survive the drop. She decided to leave him where he was, although it broke her heart. If she was to lose, at least Benjie wouldn't live with the horror of seeing it. Or be a witness. It would protect him. In those few seconds, she saw a life she was no longer part of: Tom was in his black suit, holding his son after his wife's funeral. Then a vision of Tom sitting on the sofa alone, staring at the photo of them on their wedding day. And Luna was sitting on the front windowsill, waiting for his mum to come back to him.

No, she wasn't having that. And where was Luna? He had better not hurt him. Hayley kissed Benjie on the top of his head and looked around for a weapon. All the toys were too light, too large, or too noisy. She knew if she picked up the bus or the plane it would noisily spring to life. And if she was going to win, it would have to be a surprise attack. But she knew Brandon was hoping for the same.

Then she saw the dinosaur money box she had got the day she bought the parrot. It felt good and heavy. With every penny that Tom had dropped in, he had, unknowingly, been saving their lives.

Hayley whispered to Benjie, "Mummy will be right back, sweetie."

She listened at the door to see where Brandon might be. The fourth step up always creaked, and she hadn't heard it yet. She'd told Tom they should do something about it. She never would again. Hayley opened the door and wondered why she had never noticed the noise it made as it brushed the carpet. Hopefully, he hadn't heard. The stairs were to the left, and she couldn't be sure he wasn't creeping up them. She tightened her hold on the dinosaur, ready to swing as soon as she saw him. But there was no one there.

She slipped off her slippers and prepared to descend. She couldn't just wait at the top; it was too close to the nursery. Benjie might cry out, and he would know she wasn't on her own. And what if Tom came home and walked in the door with a smile on his face like he always did, unprepared for any attack? So she went down one step at a time, listening as she went.

Damn, she was wrong—it was the fifth step that creaked. He must have heard that too. A shadow appeared at the bottom, and she knew Brandon Harding was there, waiting. Hayley could see the shadow of the arrow held above his head. She went down one more, ready to strike first herself. But she didn't get a chance. The shadow was suddenly Brandon himself, standing in front of her. He would get the first strike.

As Brandon looked up at the woman, three things happened. He felt a searing pain as a wild cat launched itself at the fleshy part of his leg, digging its claws and teeth in. Then a lump of what looked like pink crystal floated on its own towards him and hit the side of his head with force. And before everything went black, the last thing he saw was a tyrannosaurus rex coming towards his eyes.

Although he couldn't feel it, Abigail stamped on him. "Don't you ever touch our Hayley again. Good job he's not dead, or I'd kill him."

Hayley sat back on the stairs and held her head.

"I told Tom that crystals were lucky. Thank you, Suzie. I thought I was going to die." She got up, ran upstairs, and held Benjie tight. "Mummy's here, sweetheart. Mummy will never leave you. Let's go and phone Daddy."

"Daddy is not going to be very pleased with you, Hayley," said Abigail.

"I know. But we had no idea it was him for sure. He must have seen me outside the shop. But I won't tell Tom that. Alex Anderson is going to be mad he couldn't get the reward. He was so close to him last night and hadn't got a clue. Mind you, I didn't until you thought it might be him."

"But we didn't know about Molly then."

"So you're still the top detective, hun. I get a feeling we haven't seen the last of Alex. When he finds out I was responsible for Brandon's capture, we might have made an enemy."

"If he makes an enemy of you, he'll be sorry," said Suzie.

"My little protector. Thank you, sweetheart. And you, Luna. I'll never shout at you again. How did you know he was coming here?" asked Hayley.

"We didn't at first. We followed him, thank goodness. Although I think you can take care of yourself. Death by dinosaur—that would have been a first."

"Is he dead?" Hayley asked shakily.

"No, luckily for him. He wouldn't have needed to go to hell—I would have been it," said Abigail.

"That's good. I'd better ring Tom before he comes round then. I've got a lot of explaining to do, again," Hayley sighed.

Chapter 34

BACK AT GOREBRIDGE POLICE STATION, EVERYBODY was talking about the arrest of Brandon Harding. The doctor had checked him and said he was okay to be questioned. But first he put a bandage around his head to cover the wound on the side and the one between his eyes.

The Chief Constable had actually gone to the station to get a report from DCI Johnson, who didn't know much himself. He had no idea why Bennett's house should be targeted, other than the victim lived in Becklesfield. Although secretly he knew exactly why that interfering old witch had been attacked. He'd felt like it himself a few times.

"But I can say, sir, that we now have the weapon that killed Molly Travis and your friend's daughter, Felicity Fortescue. I've sent Sergeant Mills there to give them the good news."

"I'm pleased about that, well done," said George Carson.

"Tests have to be done on the arrow, but Dr Malik thinks it's from the same set. And we went to his house and found the bow and five arrows from the set of eight. I don't think there's any doubt. The lads are there searching now. And our Tom was already checking on Brandon Harding's police record like I asked him to before the attack on Mrs Bennett even happened," lied Johnson.

"And did he have one?"

"He'd been cautioned for firing a catapult at swans on the river."

"The devil," said Carson. "He should have been locked away for that. And you'll question him yourself, will you?"

"I'll be doing that as soon as my sergeant gets back, sir. Unless you'd like to sit in?"

"No, I don't think so. I'm going to ring my wife. As you know, she's very friendly with the Fortescues and Mrs Bennett, and I want to assure her that she's fine. Quite amazing how she apprehended Harding single-handed."

"Amazing," said Johnson through gritted teeth.

The Chief Constable got up to leave. "Tell young Bennett to have as much time off as he likes with his wife. Congratulations on the arrest, Tony. Keep me informed."

"Sir." All in all, not a bad result then, thought Johnson. Two high-profile murders solved, no Bennett for a few days, and best of all, he'd now got the one who had killed the beautiful girl, Molly, who reminded him of his little sister. He'd make sure they threw away the key. And he knew some people in jail who owed him a favour. Hopefully, in this case, life would mean life.

"Interview commencing at 9.33 pm. Present are Detective Chief Inspector Johnson, Sergeant Mills, duty solicitor Angus McCloud, and the defendant, Brandon James Harding. Can you confirm that's your full name, sir?"

"Yes," he mumbled.

"Please speak up for the tape."

"Yes, I said."

"Do you know why you've been arrested today?"

"I'm guessing it's because I broke into that policeman's

house, because his wife has been harassing me and I wanted to ask her why."

"I don't think that's quite right, do you? I can tell you that it's because you were found with the weapon most likely used to kill Felicity Fortescue and Molly Travis."

"I knew Molly from school, but that's all. And I've never heard of Felicity Fort, or whatever her name is."

"We had a tip to check at Lord's cricket ground on their CCTV for a certain day. Seems you went there with someone for the first day of a Test match recently."

Brandon rubbed his nose. "I've never been there. I don't even like cricket. It's boring enough on the telly, let alone sitting there all day."

"We'll see, won't we, Sergeant? It shouldn't take long to check for a certain day in August. And if you're sitting with Miss Fortescue, you'll have some explaining to do. Especially if it turns out that she bought the tickets on her credit card."

Brandon shrugged and looked at his watch.

"So let's go back to the day she was murdered. Where were you?"

"I checked, I was at work. All day."

"Someone told us that you sometimes go home for lunch. Is that right?"

"Occasionally, not very often."

"So you could have made it to Ridgeway Wood and back in time."

Brandon smiled. "Actually, I couldn't. I don't drive and it would take too long to walk. And I think if I was going to murder someone, I wouldn't have taken the bus."

"Unluckily for you, someone told us that you have a bike and can get up quite a speed. Funnily enough, that same person said you'd hidden it in a bush by the village green when you attacked Mrs Bennett."

That shocked him. "Who told you that? I don't own a bike."

Johnson looked at Mills, who shrugged. "Another tip, sir. But it has his fingerprints all over it."

"And last Monday, when Molly Travis was killed, where were you then?"

"I was at work all day, then got changed and went straight to a meeting of the Becklesfield Loves Birds. Which is not what you think. It's a birdwatching club that I go to. You can ask anyone. I was there well before it started. I helped my father to set up by getting the tables and chairs out. Actually, I was there when Mrs Bennett arrived. So I'm right; she has been harassing me. She should be arrested."

"I can't arrest someone for going to a club, however boring. Sergeant Mills, could you remind me of where Felicity Fortescue was found?"

"She was found in a bird hide, sir. Which is used by birdwatchers to watch birds so the birds can't watch them."

"Very well put. So all the birdwatchers at your BLB would know about them, Mr Harding."

"Exactly. We have over a hundred members. They might not go to the meetings, but they would know about them."

"I'm not very good at statistics, son, but I'm wondering what the likelihood of any of them owning a bow and arrow and knowing the girl that was found there is. I'd say it's not very likely at all. So for that murder at least, it's means and opportunity. I'm not sure of the motive yet, but I'm guessing she dumped you for someone better."

"If you want motive, I can give you motive," said Brandon with a sneer. "I don't know if anyone mentioned him, but she'd been seeing someone called Rex Dubois."

"Is that right? But hang on, I thought you didn't know the girl."

Brandon squirmed in his seat and said, "I don't know her. But I've heard of her. That's right, my sister follows her online. She told me."

"I think you told us you had never heard of Felicity. Shall we play the tape back, sir?"

"Don't bother. It just came to me, I'd forgotten."

"So what makes you think that Rex killed her?"

"She'd posted that they'd split and he wouldn't leave her alone. So my sister said. And I know that he's big in archery. Reckons he's good enough to go to the next Olympics. So there you go. Means, motive and opportunity. You just need the proof."

"But he was driving back from Eastbourne, where he'd won a medal. And we have the time he left his fancy hotel."

"But did you know he drives a supercar and he's been done for speeding?"

"We did. But I'm wondering how you did. You say you don't know Felicity, but you seem to know an awful lot about her ex. I'll tell you what I think, lad. I think she went out with you on the rebound. I mean, she couldn't have picked anyone more different from him. Perhaps that was the idea. She wanted a break from the usual good-looking, rich, successful blokes that could give her everything. I'm betting that she never wanted to put your picture online like she did the others. I bet it was her idea not to tell her parents about you. They wouldn't have approved, would they?"

Mills knew that Johnson was doing what he did best: riling people up till they cracked. He'd seen it before with tougher blokes than this one.

"We've met Rex Dubois, haven't we, Sergeant? He was at the Fortescues'. He had his arms around her mum, consoling her. Such a nice lad. And very handsome. Apparently, he was the son they never had. They thought the world of him and always hoped they would get married. And they say that she'd told them that she was going to patch things up again before she was killed."

"No way, you don't know anything."

"We were there, lad, when Rex told them that they were talking about getting married. She'd even chosen the ring. He was everything they ever wanted in a son-in-law. Manners, class, and could keep her in…"

"They know nothing about it!" shouted Brandon, as his solicitor advised him to calm down. "They didn't know what Rex was like. I was there when she found out he'd cheated on her for the second time. She'd actually caught him. I met her in Ridgeway Wood feeling suicidal. She looked so sad, and we got talking. She said I was like no one she'd met before. Everyone else wanted her for what she could do for them. After that, she'd pick me up after work, and we'd just drive. Once we hired a boat on the Thames. It was the best day of my life."

"But you must have known it wouldn't last? I feel for you, I really do. I could tell her dad wouldn't have approved. You would have done all right for me as a son-in-law, but I know what these snooty types are like. I expect Felicity started cooling off a bit. Probably didn't pick you up like she promised. Maybe she didn't even do you the courtesy of dumping you. Cut you off cold turkey. She'd moved on with Rex. You could never compete with him."

"I dumped her! I told her to meet me at Ridgeway Wood, and I told her it was over." Brandon's shoulders relaxed for the first time.

"So what happened, son?" Johnson said gently.

"I asked her to meet me for the last time where we'd first met. I said I had something special planned and had a present for her. With all her money, she loved presents. She wanted a hint, and I said it was something from a Roman god that money couldn't buy. That got her more intrigued. So I sent her Cupid's arrow. She would never have had anyone that loved her more than me. Rex would break her heart again and again. It was my last act of love."

Johnson wasn't gentle anymore. "I'm thinking if that's love,

I'm a Dutchman. You didn't send her Cupid's arrow. You killed her. You were a right little sneak because you wanted us to think that Rex had killed her, didn't you? You wanted him to rot in a cell. You knew that she loved him. They were the true lovers. You were just a distraction for a while. So you followed her and shot her in the back like the coward you are."

"Stop talking," his solicitor told him.

"So what happened with Molly Travis? Did she spurn your advances as well? She's another one who would have been too good for you."

"She would have said yes if I'd have fancied her. She spoke to me as I was on my way to work and said she'd seen me the day of the murder. I'd heard about the reward by then. She was trying to find out what day it was, and she didn't mention the reward, so she must have known. I said I was busy, but I agreed to meet her in the woods later. She was hiding something, and I couldn't take the chance." He put his head in his hands. "I don't know how this has happened to me."

"That's women for you," said Johnson.

"No. I don't know how I got caught, Inspector. How was the body found so quickly? No one had been near that hut for years. I wanted Rex to suffer and be under suspicion for longer than that. And any evidence of mine to be gone. The news said an old lady had found it. An old lady couldn't get anywhere near there. The nettles would have been higher than her. And how did the Bennett woman know it was me at the meeting?" Brandon shook his head in confusion. And it was almost like she was waiting for me at her house. And I knew I was on my own downstairs, so who threw the crystal?"

"I'm not sure she did know it was you at the meeting. You're sounding a bit paranoid there," said Johnson.

"Okay, there was no one about when I used the bike to go to Church Lane. No one saw me, so how could you find the bike? Or know I'd been to the cricket? You said a tip. Who?"

"We can't divulge that. We put it down to good police work, don't we, Sergeant?"

"What happens now?" Brandon asked.

"You'll be formally charged, and you won't be getting bail, I can assure you of that."

"Do you think I'll get life?"

Johnson smiled. "Oh yes. You know what they say, Mr Harding—a life for a life."

Chapter 35

IN THE END, TOM ONLY HAD ONE DAY OFF, AS HE HAD been summoned to see the Chief Constable and was given a formal commendation for his work in catching Brandon Harding. Carson had also sent a bouquet of flowers for Hayley to help her get over her ordeal. Tom hadn't been quite so sympathetic. Once he knew she was all right, he shouted at her for putting herself and his son in danger. But then he held her tight.

Hayley lied again and said she had no idea why Brandon had gone to their house, and that he was probably looking for Tom. She thought at the time that Brandon had recognised her as she stood outside the insurance shop. But what Tom didn't know wouldn't hurt him, even though it nearly did her.

Hayley wondered what would have happened if she hadn't gone in the charity shop that day and bought the dinosaur money box when she got the parrot. Although she felt bad when she thought that it was ironic that Mr Harding had sold her the weapon that was used to knock his son out. But she put that from her mind to concentrate on the parrot instead.

Hayley only hoped they weren't too late to save the man's life with all that had happened. The voice had said this time next week he would be dead, so she had arranged to meet Terry and Abigail at the charity shop as soon as Tom had left for work.

As she went out the front door, she saw a large car stop outside. She recognised it as being the same Range Rover SUV that had been parked next to her at the Becklesfield Golf Club. Oscar Fortescue and Fiona got out and walked up the path.

"You don't know us, Mrs Bennett, but we'd like to talk to you," she said.

"You're Felicity's family. Come in. I'm going out, but it can wait."

"Thank you. It's Oscar and Fiona, if it's no trouble. I can see you have your hands full. What a lovely little boy."

"Benjie's no trouble. He'll be all right in his pushchair. Do sit down."

Fiona was doing all the talking, as if her husband didn't want to be there. He was thinking that he had seen her somewhere.

"We got your address from the Chief Constable's wife, Mrs Carson. She told us that you actually caught this man. I believe he attacked you too."

"He broke in here, and there was no way I was going to let him near Benjie."

Oscar said, "A lioness looking after her cub. I admire you for that. So we think that you should have the reward, Mrs Bennett."

"My husband is one of the policemen working on the case, so I don't think I should. I know his DCI wouldn't approve. If you think I deserve it, then I volunteer to give it to Molly Travis's mother. Grieving is hard enough without having money worries. And she lost her husband last year. It would make life slightly better for her. And if she didn't want to touch the money, she could start a charity in her daughter's name."

"That is a good idea," said Fiona. "Also, Mrs Carson told me that you got involved in the case because of your gift. I hear you've done some remarkable things. Oscar doesn't believe in anything spiritual, especially since we lost Felicity."

"Never have believed in that hocus-pocus. No doubt it was your husband that you got the information from."

Hayley said, "I'm sorry you don't believe. I think we can all benefit from knowing that there's something better somewhere."

"Poppycock. When you're dead, you're dead. You'll be saying Felicity sends us a message next," he snapped.

"I wish she would, Oscar. I'd love nothing better than to give her our love and say goodbye. Are you sure you can't, Mrs Bennett? I'd love to speak to her one last time," Fiona pleaded.

"I'm sorry, she's not here."

"Don't be ridiculous, Fiona. I don't want you going all funny."

Hayley was going to enjoy this. "But there is someone that wants to talk to you, Oscar. She's got a fringe and her hair is pulled back each side. Wearing a white embroidered dress. Her name is Zoe."

Fiona gasped, and Oscar stiffened.

"Zoe, Oscar. That's his sister. She died of cancer six years ago. Now you believe, don't you?"

"She could know somehow. I'm sure the police looked into our families as part of the investigation."

"Zoe said you always were a pain in the bum, Ossy," Hayley passed on. "So prim and proper. But she says she can remember the time you picked the neighbour's best roses to give to Mum on her birthday. And you and Billy Lowry tied a bell on the tail of her cat."

"I never did that! Or did I? Yes, I did. I'd forgotten about that."

"And she says you weren't so fancy in those days. You and she were poor. Your mum couldn't afford fish and chips, but you always had a chip butty on a Friday. But they were the happiest days of her life."

Oscar shut his eyes. "I miss her so much. I didn't see enough of her in the years before she died."

"Zoe said you were the best big brother anyone could have. And she's so sorry about Felicity. She hates that you're having to grieve again. But she has a message to give you if you want it."

Fiona said, "Please, we must know."

"Zoe took your beautiful Felicity to the light. She is peaceful and all her worries are behind her. She said to tell Daddy to look after Mummy and she'll see you both on the other side. And you needn't worry about her anymore."

"We always will," sniffed Fiona.

"I'm not sure what Zoe means, Oscar, but she says you should be honest with Fiona. She would understand."

"What's she talking about, Oscar? What have you done?"

Hayley had to say, "He hasn't done anything, Fiona. I think it's that he hasn't been honest about where he comes from, is that right?"

"We were poor, Fiona. I didn't come from money like I told you. We were so poor, I made sure I never would be again."

"It wouldn't have mattered. But you've always made a point of looking down your nose. How could you?"

Hayley said, "I think I understand. You were frightened of people looking down on you first. The little boy with the bad haircut and the trousers that were too short, or the second-hand shirt that was too big. I'm sorry, Oscar. Children can be cruel."

"There's a lot I have to tell you, my dear." He would be pleased to share things with his wife. It was almost a weight off his mind. "And you, Mrs Bennett, I'm sorry I doubted you. I was going to get my solicitor to send a cheque to Molly's mother, but I think we should pay a visit. We may be able to help." Hayley knew that he didn't want to face Mrs Travis. He knew that if he hadn't offered the reward, Molly might still be alive.

She would have loved to have told him that the only one to blame was Brandon Harding. "We'll leave you to get on with what you were going to do, Hayley."

"I have to pay a private detective we hired as well. I think he was hoping he could get the reward," said Fiona.

"That's another puzzle solved as well. I have a feeling he said I should have been burned at the stake and that I was weird and witchy."

"How on earth did you know that?" asked Oscar.

"A ghost friend went back to his house with him in his car and heard him say it into a recorder."

"Well, I suppose if you don't want to tell me you don't have to. It's your prerogative, of course."

Hayley didn't try to explain that she was telling the truth, as she was in a hurry. She just stood up and said, "I'm so pleased you came, but I do have something very important to do. I've got to see a man about a parrot."

Chapter 36

ABIGAIL LOOKED VERY IRRITABLE WAITING OUTSIDE the charity shop. "Where have you been, Hayley? We've got a man to save."

"I think I just did, hun," she answered, thinking about Mr and Mrs Fortescue walking to the car, hand in hand.

There were two ladies sorting some donations at the till.

"If you've come to see Mr Harding again, he's taking some time off. I expect you heard what happened."

"I have, Mrs Malloy. I feel for him, I really do. Actually, it's you I wanted to have a word with. Do you remember that parrot you sold me for Benjie? I don't suppose you know who brought it in, do you?"

"Let me think, dear. She brings some things occasionally. I don't think she's from Becklesfield. She bought something that day, I believe. I think it was another toy for her nephew that stayed with them sometimes. A jigsaw puzzle, I think. She may have paid by card. Do you want me to look?"

"Yes, please, Mrs Malloy."

"Why do you want to know? We could give you a refund, I know it was broken. Or swap it for something else."

"It wasn't that. There was something inside that belonged to her. We were hoping to return it."

"I shouldn't worry. We often find things in pockets or bags. We just throw them out or sell them on."

"This was something personal. I really think we should give it back to her. Could you check for me, please?"

"Here it is. She paid by debit card. Er, Gaynor Webster."

"I don't suppose it gives an address, does it?"

"No, but I have a feeling that she mentioned the charity shop in Little Astley. She said they didn't want to take any more toys. But I could be wrong."

"That is so helpful, thank you," said Hayley as she turned to go.

"It's bad luck to go to a charity shop and not buy anything, you know?"

"I've not heard of that before. But I'm not one to argue with the universe." So Hayley chose another cuddly toy to add to the thirty that Benjie already had.

Terry and Abigail were already full of ideas to track down Gaynor Webster of Little Astley.

"We don't know if she actually lives there yet. But most of all, we need to find out if someone close to her has died," said Hayley. "We might be too late."

"I reckon it's her husband and she put out a hit on him," said Terry.

"This isn't New York, hun."

"You're right. There are far more murders here."

"I can't ask Tom. It's a big day for him today with the CC. Let's go and buy the Chiltern Weekly and see if there's anything in there."

But there was no mention of anyone being murdered, dying or missing in the county. There was only one person who could help. Someone who had worked for the Chiltern Weekly in life, and in death had helped The Deadly Detective Agency – Celia

Hanson. She had been the paper's best journalist when she was alive and specialised in crime, deaths and inquests. And what made her such an asset was that she had an eidetic memory.

Hayley drove Terry and Abigail to Gorebridge and parked outside while they entered the newspaper's offices to find her. Celia was sitting, unseen, on the editor's desk, looking over his shoulder at his screen. She was delighted to see her fellow ghosts.

"Hello there. What can I do for you?"

"We want to know if there have been any deaths connected to a woman called Gaynor Webster in the last week or so. So it could be Mr Webster."

"Tell me all of it. Let's go and find somewhere more comfortable."

They found an empty office along the corridor.

Abigail explained, "So this woman was overheard telling someone that, 'By this time next week, hopefully he'll be dead'."

"I see. And who heard that?" asked Celia.

"It might sound strange, but it was a parrot."

"With you lot, why would it sound strange?"

"Really?"

"Of course I think it's strange. Even for you. When was this supposed to have happened?"

Terry said, "Sometime this week. We're hoping not yet. And we think she's from Little Astley."

"Okay, let me think, guys." Celia closed her eyes and looked up. "Cyril Webster died March the 10th, 2009. Jon Webster; drugs overdose, December the 15th, 2016. No, that's it."

"Well that's that then," said Abigail, disappointed.

"Hold on, I haven't finished yet. Um, I know one of the reporters was at the police station last night and happened to overhear that a woman had phoned to say her husband hadn't returned home. Her name was Jenny Parnell."

"But that could be anything, Celia. But thanks for trying."

"Ah, but I happen to remember that she lived in Little Astley."

Chapter 37

Hayley Moon, not Hayley Bennett, pulled up outside the large house in Clarence Crescent in Little Astley. Benjie was with his godmother and Terry and Abigail were in the back of the car.

Jenny Parnell was looking out of the window, where she had spent most of her time since Rory hadn't come home. This woman looked a bit like a witch in her long skirt and black hair, but when she had phoned, she seemed to be the only one who believed something was wrong. Jenny rested her hand on her belly. They had only just found out they were expecting their first child and they were both overjoyed. There was no way Rory would have left her voluntarily. Hayley Moon thought there was something wrong, and she ran some sort of agency. She was the only hope Jenny had at the present.

"Come in, Hayley. You don't know how happy I was to get your call. The police didn't seem interested at all. They said it was too soon to be thought of as a missing person."

"When is the baby due, Jenny?"

"How did you know about that? I'm not showing, am I?"

"No, hun. It's just a talent I have."

"I've got another seven months to go. Rory was so excited, so I knew he would come home if he could."

"So what happened yesterday? Tell me from the beginning."

Jenny blew out her cheeks. "I went to see my mum. She lives about a two-hour drive from here. Rory works from home and I said goodbye at about nine o'clock in the morning. And when I got back at sixish, he wasn't here. He'd wanted me to stay the night at Mum's because he worried about me driving all that way there and back."

"Could there have been a reason for that?"

"Like what? You mean like a woman he wanted to see last night? No, I'll never believe that."

"I had to ask. I don't think he did either. Have you tried his phone?"

"It's turned off. And none of his friends have heard from him."

Hayley went and stared at their wedding photo on the wall. She touched it and felt nothing but affection.

"Have you got anything of his that I could take with me? I might get a feeling of where he is."

"Like a jumper?"

Abigail laughed, "She thinks you're like a tracker dog, Hayl."

"No, hun. Something hard that he used every day. Something metal maybe?"

"Excuse me, I'll look in our bedroom."

That gave Hayley a chance to ask the two spirits, "What do you think?"

Abigail said, "I think she's scared. As much as she believes he wouldn't go, she knows there's a chance of it."

Jenny returned and passed Hayley a small silver box. "His grandmother gave him this when he started his company. It's to put his business cards in."

"That's perfect." Hayley ran her fingers over it. "I'll find out the truth, but I can't promise it's the outcome you pray for, Jenny."

"At this point, I just need to know."

"Could you think of anywhere he could have gone? What did he enjoy doing?"

"He played golf, liked fishing, although he hadn't done that for years. Liked to walk to the pub in the village for a drink. But I've rung all his friends and they have no idea where he is either. So do what you have to and I'll pay anything you ask. I can write a cheque now."

"That won't be necessary. Let's see what I can do for you first. This might sound strange, but do you know anyone called Webster, Gaynor Webster?"

Jenny looked puzzled. "Of course, that's his business partner. Why do you ask?"

Hayley opened the card holder and looked at one of the cards.

WEBPAR

Software Developers

Programming & Design

Call Gaynor WEBster & Rory PARnell

"Her name came to me so she could be important. Send me her address, Jenny. I'll need to talk to her."

"I already have. She says she has no idea. As far as she knew they were both having yesterday off."

"Still send me her address and number, please. So I'll take this case with me and get back to you as soon as I can. And try not to worry. The people I work with are amazing."

"I hope so. This was the happiest week of his life and I'd hate it to be his last."

"Because of the baby?"

"And because he'd written some software that would make him and Gaynor millionaires."

"Is that right?" said Hayley thoughtfully, with a look at Terry and Abigail.

Chapter 38

ABIGAIL COULDN'T UNDERSTAND WHY THEY DIDN'T just find Gaynor, but Hayley told her that whatever she had done, was done. The most important thing was to find Rory. He could still be alive. She felt a sense of that when she held the silver case. So they went back to Church Lane and Hayley told them to get the others and come back in an hour, not before. She had something she needed to do first.

When they did come back, they found Hayley lying on her bed, surrounded by candles and a tortoiseshell cat. On her chest she was holding the silver case.

They stood there for a moment, not knowing if she was asleep.

"I know you're there, you know?"

"Good," said Abigail. "Where is he?"

"It doesn't work like that." Hayley sat up, disturbing Luna, who wasn't pleased. "It's good news and bad news. I feel he's still alive, but not for much longer. I'm struggling to breathe when I touch this. I only see blackness."

"Anything else, dear?"

"Not much, Betty. I hear wind, like it's moving trees. Water dripping and hitting something hard. Like it does if you have a leak."

"So is he in some sort of old building, do you think?" said Abigail.

"Could be, or under a tree. I can smell something as well. It's not nice; something rotting."

"I hope it's not decomposition," said Lillian. "Although, even if he died yesterday, that wouldn't be occurring yet."

"I don't think it's human, hun. More like food that's gone off. Like rancid meat or something."

Terry had a thought. "Or fish!"

"Yes, like fish. That could be it. Let me ring Jenny. Jenny, you said Rory used to like to fish, do you know where he went? Thank you. I'll keep you posted."

"Well?" said Abigail impatiently.

"He used to go to the trout farm in Kimberly and the River Gore at Ottersmill. We'll go to the river first."

"Do you have a feeling, dear?"

"No, hun, it's nearer."

As they drove up the lane to the river, Hayley did begin to get a feeling. Someone or something was guiding her. She walked to the towpath and they saw fishermen in both directions.

"He could be anywhere," said Betty. "Suzie and I can go this way and look."

"Which way do you think, Hayl?" asked Abigail.

She got the silver case out of her pocket and held it in both hands. "Left. I think left." She went up to one of the anglers and asked if he had been there yesterday. He hadn't. They carried on until they came to a weeping willow tree that was rustling in the wind. Just like the sound she had heard. She parted the low branches and smelled the same rancid smell as well.

"Here, guys. He's here."

Rory Parnell was lying on his back in a bed of reeds with

dried blood coming from a gash on his head. A fishing rod had been thrown on top of him. It looked like they were too late. There was shimmering over him as if his soul were leaving his mortal body.

Hayley knelt down and tried to remember the course she had done before she had Benjie. First she checked he wasn't breathing, then tilted his head back and blew. Luckily, Lillian was there to talk her through it. She then started to pump the chest to the beat of Staying Alive that she had seen somewhere.

After a while they saw his eyes flicker and his chest go up and down, so Hayley rang for an ambulance and the police. Rory was still unconscious, but at least he was breathing.

"He's so lucky," said Lillian. "Another few minutes and he would have been dead."

"I have a feeling it wasn't just luck, hun. Someone was looking after him up there."

"And down here," said a voice.

"You're his grandmother," said Hayley sweetly. "You gave him the silver case."

"Yes. It's funny how things work out. I saw it in your hand."

"Jenny gave it to me and it led me here. Have you been here all the time?"

"I didn't see it happen, but Rory called out to me as he lay dying. He passed once and I told him to go back. I said he had to be there for Jenny and his baby girl. I told him help was on the way. And then you came."

"Do you know who did this to him? Whoever it was wanted everyone to think that he was fishing and fell and hit his head on that rock. This was no accident."

"I didn't see it, but I saw the man who did it," said Rory's grandmother.

Abigail said, "A man? We thought it might be his business partner, Gaynor."

"She was there. But it was her husband that did it. She was

laughing as he dragged my poor Rory and hid him here. She carried the rock and fishing rod over. They said they didn't think he'd be found for days."

"I have a feeling this was all for money, so they needed a body at some point. Obviously after all the evidence had gone," said Abigail. "You should be so proud of yourself, you saved your grandson's life."

"It was never his time. I knew someone would come. Who are you, by the way?"

"The Deadly Detective Agency," said Lillian proudly, as they heard the siren and saw the flashing blue light, followed by two police cars.

Chapter 39

JOHNSON, ONCE AGAIN, WAS CONFUSED. "I SWEAR TO God, if that Bennett and his wife have anything to do with this I'll…"

But then the Chief Constable phoned and congratulated him on saving a man from certain death.

"Just doing my duty, sir. I've made sure Mr and Mrs Webster were arrested. The victim couldn't say anything, but I made sure our best man, PC Bennett, went with him to the hospital in case he comes round. We're going to question them now. I'll tell you if we charge them today. Thank you, sir."

"Sergeant! Put them in interview rooms, separately."

Mills had brought them in an hour ago and it was obvious who wore the trousers, and it wasn't Colin Webster. If he tried to talk, Gaynor would tell him to shut up. So they decided to break him first.

Johnson started by giving him a false smile. "Colin, are you aware that we found Rory Parnell by the river at Ottersmill?"

"I wasn't until you dragged me out of my home. I knew he was missing because Jenny had rung us. We told her we didn't have a clue where he was. We had nothing to do with his death."

"Who said he's dead?"

"I, I just assumed. He's not dead?" Colin said worriedly. "So you dragged me and my poor terrified wife here for nothing?"

"Poor terrified wife? That's not how my sergeant would describe her. I'd say that's more you. So how do you know Rory?"

"He and my wife run a company; WebPar. It's to do with programming."

"And are they successful?"

"They do okay. They both work from home, so they don't make enough to pay for an office, but they pay themselves a fair wage."

"What would happen to the business if, say, one of them died, or were, for example, attacked and left for dead?" said Johnson with a straight face.

"That's not what happened. But if one of them died the other would get the business. They had a solicitor draw it up when they first started. That's standard business practice, Inspector. If anything happened to Gaynor, then Rory would inherit."

"So it's rather a shame that it looks like Rory is going to make it. I have a constable sitting by his bedside and I've heard he's awake and about to make a statement," Johnson lied. "I'm just waiting for a call. One of my colleagues is talking to your wife, and I'm guessing she's going to throw you under the bus. The first one to talk will get a better deal, won't they, Sergeant? I reckon she's going to say that it was your idea. We already know you're the one that did it. You were seen. So if you want to spend the rest of your life in jail then that's fine. But I'm guessing it was the wife's idea. You don't seem the type to me, Colin. Am I right?"

"It wasn't us. You have no proof. I'm guessing he got a brain injury when he was hit on the head. Even if he says we were there, it'll never stand up in court."

Johnson sighed. "Oh, Colin, Colin, Colin. I almost feel sorry for you. Sergeant, did I say the victim was hit on the head?"

"No, sir, you didn't."

"Someone told me. It must have been one of the other policemen."

"I can assure you that they wouldn't have. They know what I would do to them."

"That's true, Mr Webster," said Mills. "The only way you could have known that was if you were there. And according to one source there was a witness. You hit Rory and dragged him under the tree, and your wife put the stone next to his head and threw the fishing rod and fish on him."

"Rubbish, there was no one there."

"Oh, dear, Colin, is that correct? No wonder your wife could talk you into this. You're a bit thick, aren't you? I bet your wife is in there now saying how it was your idea. Go and check, Mills."

Mills pretended to talk to the other inspector and went back in.

"She's talking, sir. She says it was all his idea. Apparently, Mr Parnell had recently come up with an idea that was going to make millions. They already had a buyer for it. So it was pure greed. And her husband had no business sense, so he came up with the idea and threatened her if he didn't go along with it."

"Now that I believe," said Johnson. "Looks like your wife will be getting off lightly then. She'll probably get ten years, out in five, and can carry on living in your house. I don't suppose you'll see the light of day again. Shame, Colin, I rather liked you."

"Now wait a minute, Inspector, what if I was to tell the truth?"

"We'll see what we can do."

"Okay, it was me. But it was all her idea. She told me to get him to take me fishing. She did it for the money. I can't believe she'd talk. She made sure I knew not to."

"Ah, sorry, we made that up, Colin. We haven't got to her yet. But thank you, it's made our job a lot easier. And for your information, poor Rory Parnell is still in a bad way. The charge could well be murder. But we don't need his testimony now."

"I tried to tell her it was stupid. I hate that woman."

"I think it might be mutual. Another thing we learned is that she was known to be clearing out a lot of men's clothes lately. I wouldn't be surprised to find out that she was getting rid of you next. We might have saved your life, Colin. Don't worry, you don't need to thank us. Right, we'll go and tell your wife the good news — that you're both going to be charged with attempted murder. And you'd better hope that Rory pulls through."

Abigail, Terry and Betty all applauded. Johnson had done well.

Chapter 40

LILLIAN, SUZIE AND HAYLEY WERE STANDING BY THE bed of Rory in Gorebridge General Hospital. Hayley had promised to stay with Jenny as long as she could. Rory was awake, but feeling very weak. He was on a drip for severe dehydration, but his doctor thought that the prognosis was good.

"Rory, this is Hayley. She found you and saved your life. I'm not sure how, but she worked out that you were by the river."

"Thank you," he answered with a croaky voice.

"That's alright, we were just happy that we found you in time. They've taken your partner and her husband in for questioning. Was it him that hit you?"

"I don't know. It was Colin that said he wanted to go fishing. I don't know what happened after that. My head hurts so bad."

"Don't talk anymore, Rory," said Hayley.

"Why don't you get off. You've got a baby to see to."

"If you're sure, Jenny. If there's anything else you need just call."

"There is one thing. How did you know that there was something wrong? The police didn't know anything."

Hayley laughed. "Actually, you could say a little birdie told me," she said as they left the loving couple to spend some time together.

She walked with Lillian and Suzie down the long corridor that led to the Accident and Emergency department. Hayley tried not to look anyone in the eye, just in case it was a recently departed. She had enough trouble with the spirits she knew.

"This is where Lillian and I first met," said Suzie.

"It's a few years ago now. I'll never forget the first time I saw you. I was stuck at the hospital and when I saw you pass, I knew I would take care of you for your mum. Till she joins you anyway."

Hayley stopped walking. "You've given me an idea. With all that's gone on in the last few days, I forgot we've still got to find Gracie's family. You didn't go to Edenbury Heights with us, but Kylie just thought she was her daughter's imaginary friend. She died at least two years ago, because she was there when they moved in. Now we know she died somewhere else, but even if someone did, you might still be brought here to the A and E. Are there any spirits here that might know Lillian? I don't suppose you knew a Gracie May, did you?"

"I didn't work in A and E before I died. But since then I know there's an old matron that's been haunting the poor nurses here for at least ten years. She's a bit of a tartar, but she'll know. Doris Crookshank is her name, I think. There she is."

Matron Crookshank was shouting at a nurse who had no idea she was being reprimanded by a ghost that had been long dead.

"Nurse Whitlow, when are you going to wash your hands properly? And if I made a bed like that I would have been sacked. Hello, Lillian, how are you?"

"Fine, thanks. You remember Suzie, but this is Hayley. She's a medium and very good. But she needs your help."

"As long as she promises to come back one day. I've got a few people who want to pass on messages before they get out of my A and E. They make it look very untidy."

"Cross my heart, Matron," answered Hayley. "Can we go over there and talk? I'm trying to find a young girl's family. She's a lost soul until we do. We think she died in this area between two and ten years ago. No outward sign of death. Her name is Gracie May and she was about five or six maybe."

"Hmm, I don't remember her. There's a doctor here that would. Well, he could check the files for you. He's not dead though, but that won't matter to you, Hayley."

"But will he help us? I don't think doctors are allowed to talk about patients, are they?"

"Dr Glover will. Just tell him if he doesn't I'll tell everyone about what he got up to with Dr Vance's wife. And more disgustingly, how he treats the young nurses he should be helping. Let's say he's very hands-on. And if they spurn his advances they can lose their jobs. Mention Nurse Olsen and Nurse Whitlow for starters. I'm sure he'll tell you everything."

Matron pointed him out and Hayley went over and whispered in his ear. He ushered her over to an empty cubicle.

"That's absolute rubbish. Who told you that? I'm a respected doctor."

"And if you want that to continue, then tell me about Gracie May. The one that told me has promised to keep it to herself if you help. I only want to find her family. No one will ever know. She was a small child, aged about six. Short brown hair in a bob. She had a brother called James."

"I do remember her, actually. I'm not looking up her record, but I'll tell you what I remember. It's hard to forget. It's not often a whole family dies in an RTA."

"Her whole family died in a car accident?"

"The young girl was pronounced dead at the scene, but the mother, father and the boy died later on of their injuries. We couldn't save them."

"That explains a lot."

"But their name wasn't May. It was Fallon. I think that could have been her middle name, but it was about three years ago, so I could be wrong."

A nurse called him and he left her to think about what they had learned.

"I understand now how they got separated. But I wonder where the others went," said Hayley. "I think they're still looking or waiting for her. She remembered her house had a red roof, so maybe they stay there in case she comes home."

"At least we've got a full name now. There's bound to be something written somewhere," said Lillian.

"I didn't like that doctor at all," said Suzie. "And we can't do anything about it. We said if he talked to us we wouldn't tell anyone."

"I didn't say I wouldn't tell. It was Matron Crookshank who said she wouldn't say what he got up to if he told us about Gracie. I'm going to report Dr Glover right now."

"It was great, Abigail," Suzie told her later. "Hayley found the Ward Manager and told her everything. And it wasn't the first time she'd heard it. But now she has the names of two nurses she said she might be able to do something about it."

"Good job. Well done, Hayley. Serves him right. So can you see if you can find out anything about the accident? That is so awful. A whole family was wiped out."

"I don't like to, but I think the quickest way will be to phone Tom. That way we can get their address and exactly where the accident took place."

"Tell him it's about a child," said Abigail. "I noticed he's been a lot more helpful since he's become a father."

"He has actually. I'll stress how the little girl is all on her own with no one to love. He'll do it within the hour, you watch."

Tom actually gave Hayley the information within ten minutes.

Isla and Martin Fallon, their children, James and Grace, were killed on the Northridge Road near to Edenbury Manor. The family's address was Red Roof Farm, Northridge.

After Terry and Abigail made sure the rest of the family were actually still waiting at the farm, Hayley set off for Kylie's house at Edenbury Heights. The lovely Gracie would soon be reunited with her mummy, daddy and brother.

Chapter 41

"Come in, Hayley. I'm so glad you phoned. I've got Britney off school today. I hope that's okay."

"I think it's perfect, Kylie. She can say goodbye to Gracie. Suzie is here with me. She's a bit older than them, but she can help us." Hayley didn't mention Abigail was there as well.

"They're playing in her room at the moment. Do you want a cup of coffee?"

"Water would be great, thank you."

"Come through to the kitchen. You'd be very proud of me. I wasn't scared of having a ghost at all after I got used to it. Except at night, if I'm honest. Then I tried to keep one eye open. I didn't tell Marlon. He wouldn't have slept at all. And I didn't tell Britney anything."

"She'll just think it was her imaginary friend, and one day she won't think of her at all. Until she has her own child, then it'll come back to her. And anyway, Britney is going to be too busy with the patter of tiny feet."

"Oh, don't say that, Hayley. We weren't going to have any more kids. Not for ages anyway."

Hayley laughed. "I didn't say it was a child. Four feet, not two. Next week, to cheer Britney up, you decide to get her a little puppy from the dog rescue in Amersford."

"That sounds more like it. We always had a dog when I was growing up. Thank goodness for that. You had me worried then. So you found Gracie's family?"

"My friends Abigail and Terry found them at Red Roof Farm. It's literally two miles from here, and the accident was near there. It was pouring with rain and the car went out of control and hit a tree head-on. Gracie died immediately, and I think she must have wandered away and ended up here."

"The poor little thing."

"Would you like to see a photograph? Tom sent me one."

Kylie burst into tears. "I'm sorry. I feel for her so much. She's so small and pretty. Makes me worry even more for Britney."

Hayley put her arm around her. "But there's a happy ending. She's going to be reunited with her family. It will be as if they were never apart, I promise you. Let's go and tell her the good news."

Upstairs, Suzie smiled at the little girl with the brown bob, who she knew was Gracie. She didn't expect the other girl to see her, but she did.

"Do you want to play with me and Gracie? You can have this doll."

"I'd love to," answered Suzie.

"Britney can see Suzie as well," said Kylie.

"Children are very sensitive. Gracie, I've got some good news for you. We found Mummy and Daddy and James. They can't wait to see you."

"Can Britney come with me?"

"No. Britney has to stay with her mummy and daddy. You might be able to visit."

"But I want her to come."

"James has missed you. I said we would go and see them today."

"All right then."

Britney said, "You're not going, are you?"

Kylie hugged her daughter. "She has to see her own mummy now, darling. You have to say goodbye."

"But I don't want to."

"How about if we go and get a puppy?"

"Okay. Bye, Gracie. See you soon."

Suzie laughed. "That's charming. Come on, Gracie, take my hand. We're going to Red Roof Farm."

"I know that farm. Bye, Britney. Love you." Gracie hugged her friend, and Britney's bottom lip quivered.

"Bye, Gracie. Come back soon."

Kylie asked Hayley if she thought the little ghost would ever come back.

"No, hun, I think this is goodbye. Gracie says thank you for everything and you were a lovely mummy."

They made their way to the door, but then Gracie turned and ran back to hug Kylie's legs.

"I love you, Mummy."

"I can feel her, Hayley. Goodbye, my special little girl. I'll never forget you. Thank you for taking care of Britney."

Suzie took one of Gracie's hands and Abigail the other as they left Edenbury Heights for the next part of the young girl's journey.

Hayley drove along Northridge Road until she saw a signpost for Red Roof Farm up a lane to the right. But something else caught her eye. Before she turned, she saw a bouquet of flowers on the side of the road, in front of a clump of trees. She realised she had seen it many times before and had often wondered who had died there so tragically. Now she knew.

As they drove along the bumpy lane, Abigail gave a wry

smile. "Now Hayley, you're going to laugh when we get there. Or cry."

"Why? As long as it's got nothing to do with birds, hun. Oh, I see. Actually, that is kinda funny."

Hayley knew she wouldn't have been able to go into the farm, so she parked just outside the entrance. Under the sign that read, Red Roof Turkey *Farm*.

"You have to see the funny side," said Abigail. "You stay here. I don't want you to be done for trespassing or fowl play and be tarred and feathered."

"I just thought, Suzie could be a poultry-geist," laughed Hayley.

"Why didn't I think of that one?" said Abigail. "Come on, little Gracie, let's go and find Mummy before the jokes get worse. Do you remember this place?"

"Sort of. It looks a bit different. I'm scared, what if I don't remember them?"

"You will, hun. Go with Abigail and Suzie and we'll come back soon to see you. I promise."

Five minutes later she saw Abigail and Suzie walk back to the car. They were followed by the newly reunited family. Gracie was looking full of joy and so was her mummy. Her father, Martin Fallon, didn't look quite so happy.

"Hayley, they need to have a word with you. This is the first time that they've been able to tell anyone this. They need your help."

"I'll do what I can. What's up?"

"The accident that killed them wasn't an accident. They were deliberately murdered."

Chapter 42

IT WAS LIKE THE GUINNESS BOOK OF RECORDS; TO SEE how many ghosts you could get in a Mini. But they all got in somehow and sat outside the farm.

"Are you sure it wasn't just an accident? My husband, Tom, read the report and it said it was a very wet night. And they checked the car and there was nothing wrong with the brakes. It looks like you just skidded off the road on the bend."

"They're right, there wasn't anything wrong with the car. That's what he wanted them to think. But he caused the accident all right," Martin told them.

"Who is he?" asked Abigail.

"My brother-in-law, Nigel Knight. My sister and he own the farm now."

"But I'm sure the forensic investigators would know. How could he have done it?"

"They weren't there. It was dark that night and I was driving up the road. The windscreen wipers were going as fast as they could, but the vision was bad. But then I was blinded. Someone shone a light right in the car. It was so bright I lifted up my arm to shield my eyes and then we hit the tree and it went dark."

"It's true," said Isla. "The next thing we knew, we were all running round the hospital trying to find Gracie. We were desperate. We heard the police and the ambulance drivers talking, and they just said Martin was going too fast and missed the bend. That wasn't true."

"I hit the kerb and the car took off and went into a tree."

"Sounds like murder to me, Hayley," said Abigail.

"But hang on, it could have been someone walking along the side of the road with a torch, trying to see where they were going."

"So why weren't they there when the ambulance came?" Abigail persisted. "It would have been in the report."

Martin said, "But mainly because I know it was my light. I can show you it now. It's on the farm. We bought it to light up the land between the wood and the pens to check for foxes. One fox can kill hundreds. The turkeys panic and huddle together in a corner. I've seen it. They either suffocate or trample each other to death. It's not a normal torch. It's a hand-held spotlight with five hundred thousand candlepower. I'm telling you, that's what it was."

"I believe you, hun. The perfect murder. No one would ever know what really caused the accident. Tell me about your brother-in-law."

"His name is Nigel. My mum died years ago, and my dad ran the farm. Nigel was the foreman. Anyway, he married my sister, Rose, and they had Harry. Dad had a small cottage built for them near the farmhouse. I lived in the main house with Isla and the kids. Then Dad died of cancer about four years ago and that's when the trouble started. In the will, Rose got some money and their cottage, but I got the farm. Rose wasn't worried, but he was. Nigel thought they should have half. He tried to dispute the will but he couldn't."

"Would it be worth killing over a few turkeys?"

"A few? Try ten thousand. And he and Rose got a percentage of the profits, but that wasn't enough for him."

"I see. And I'm presuming if you died it would go to Isla. But if you both died it would go to your sister."

"Exactly, Hayley. I know you've already done so much in finding our daughter, but could you help us? I think the only reason he hasn't killed my sister is that they have Harry together. I don't trust him at all."

"Are you sure Rose had no idea of what he did?"

Isla answered, "She's the sweetest person. She was heartbroken and still puts flowers where the accident was every week. I'm from a small island in Scotland and I'm fey like you, Hayley. I love Rose, but I've never taken to Nigel. I hate the fact he's in our home now. I think we could all rest in peace if we saw him pay for what he did. Rose could sell the place and get away from the memory of our deaths. She has no interest in turkey farming, and she hates them after one nearly took her eye out."

"I'm not that keen on birds myself at the moment," confessed Hayley. "Was there no evidence at all at the inquest? Like any sign of someone being there? Or someone seeing a flash of light?"

Martin said, "Not that we know of. But we didn't go to the inquest. We were spending our time looking for Gracie. But I do remember before Nigel killed us he was talking about kids who had shone lasers at planes and they were in trouble for blinding the pilots."

"That's where he got the idea from then. Where had you been the night you died?"

"It was a Sunday evening. Every other week Isla would take the kids to visit her mum in Bournemouth. Then they'd get the train home, which got them back to Halton Thorpe at 6.35. I'd always go and pick them up. I'm wondering how many times he waited there for just the right time on a dark evening."

"He would have had to make sure there were no other cars about as well. That night he hit the jackpot: no cars and it was pouring with rain. The perfect murder at the perfect time," said Hayley.

"I know there's no reason that you should, but do you think you can help us? We won't be able to rest while he's still free," said Isla.

"What do you think, Abigail? No witnesses, no evidence, and not even a motive we can prove. After all, it went to his wife, not him."

"Nothing at all going for it, no suspicious circumstances, and it happened years ago; sounds just like my sort of case. If it wasn't difficult, it wouldn't be so interesting. We just need to come up with a plan. I think we'll call it Operation Cold Case. No, Operation Cold Turkey."

"Brilliant, hun. Okay then," said Hayley. "We'd better get back. Martin, you stay here and watch Nigel like a hawk, or even a turkey. If anything happens, or if you're worried, go to the Becklesfield Public Library. One of us will be there. And forget about the accident for a while. You're all together for the first time. Go and enjoy it. Bye, Gracie, I'm so happy for you. Right, I'm going to need Tom's help again. Let's hope he's in a good mood."

Tom was shocked to hear that a whole family had been killed in an appalling way just for greed.

"But I looked at the report and there was no sign of the vehicle being tampered with. The brakes and everything were checked."

"You imagine driving on a dark night and someone suddenly shines a spotlight in your eyes. You're totally blinded."

"I know, love. But it's going to be a devil to prove."

"Who did the report? Do you think he's still working there?"

"Er, it was Arthur Hill. He still works for Traffic. I'll talk to him tomorrow if I get the chance. I'm sure he'll remember the case and want to help. God knows how I'll tell him I think there's something wrong."

"You'll think of something, hun. You always do."

The following evening after work, Tom was pleased to tell Hayley that Arthur had been more than happy to talk about it.

"I asked him if he remembered the accident, and he said he'll never be able to forget it. There were some things that didn't add up for him either. He said it looked like Martin Fallon hadn't seen the bend, even though he'd done the journey loads of times. And there were no black tyre marks from suddenly braking on the road. He even wondered if he had deliberately driven into the tree."

"It definitely wasn't that. Thank goodness they didn't try to blame Martin," said Hayley. "That would have rubbed salt in."

"The verdict at the inquest was accidental deaths. Because it didn't sit right with Arthur, he went back the next day after it happened and found there were a lot of footprints next to the trees. Because it had been dry before that he thought they had probably been made that night. He thought they looked like they had been made by wellington boots."

"That would be right for a farmer. Did he take casts?"

"No. Everyone else thought it was an accident. And he said he wished he'd picked up the cigarette butts that were there. But you know what it's like, a PC doesn't get a lot of time."

"That really helps, Tom. Nigel Knight won't know the police didn't keep them as evidence."

"Don't you go to that farm, Hayley. I've already nearly lost you this month."

"Nope. This is definitely for the ghosts. I'm not even going to talk to his wife, Rose. If she starts to get suspicious, it might put her in danger. No, I'm keeping well away from this one. But

I'll help from home. Operation Cold Turkey is all down to the rest of The Deadly Detective Agency."

"I can't see how they're going to do it. It's not like he's going to confess after all this time, is he?"

"You never know, hun. Abigail has been working on a plan that includes cunning, precision timing, and the supernatural."

Chapter 43

THE FIRST PART OF OPERATION COLD TURKEY involved Hayley paying a visit to Lady Caroline at Chiltern Hall. Before she moved to the manor house, she had lived in London and performed in various theatres. Abigail wanted to put that to good use, and Hayley asked Caroline to record various sentences in a Scottish accent to sound like Isla. And they asked her where they could buy fake blood — the type you would use in amateur dramatics.

Back at the farm, Martin was giving Lillian and Suzie a guided tour, in particular the place where the deadly spotlight, the telephones, and Nigel's office were.

Terry and Betty were to keep close to Rose and her son, and to note what they did and at what time. If the plan was to work, it had to be done when Nigel was on his own and no danger or suspicion could be cast on his wife. Abigail, of course, was supervising.

By the following Monday morning, all was in place.

Rose Knight took her son, Harry, to the car and they drove to his school, whereafter she went to do her weekly shop at the supermarket in Northridge.

In Nigel's office, the telephone rang on his desk.

"Red Roof Farm."

"I know what you did, Nigel," said a Scottish voice.

"Who's this?"

"Isla."

The tormenting of Nigel Knight had begun.

Immediately after he had slammed the phone down, there was a tap at the window. Hovering in mid-air was a pair of green wellingtons covered in blood. Nigel ran to the door, but they had gone. He saw them later, standing by the back door where he had left them, covered only in mud.

Terry asked Abigail, "Are you trying to get him to confess or kill himself?"

"Either works for me. But people will always remember Martin for driving too fast or dangerous driving, so it should come out, I reckon."

"So what's next?"

"You've found out that Rose goes to bed first and he sits drinking in the sitting room. So tonight's the perfect time to do part two."

Nigel was getting tired and was just going to turn the television off when his mobile rang. It was not a number he recognised.

"Hello."

"This is Isla again, Nigel. You remember me. I'm looking at the light you used to kill my family. I'm coming for you, Nigel."

"Hello, hello. Who is this?"

Nigel sat for a moment and thought whoever it was must be outside by the turkey pens. He unlocked his cupboard and took out his shotgun. He listened at the bottom of the stairs. Rose was asleep.

He put his boots on and crept out into the night. He jumped when he saw two eyes looking at him, but then realised it was the cat. The moon was full so he could see without a torch, and he wanted to surprise whoever was trying to blackmail him. But as he got closer, he could see no one was there. Just when he was giving up and going back in, the light switched on, blinding him.

"Who's that? Turn it off, or else I'll shoot."

The light went off. But Nigel could still see the brilliance of it for ages afterwards. As his eyes got used to the dark, he knew there was no one there. The spotlight was powered by batteries, so someone had to move the switch on the side.

"Next time I'll let you have both barrels. You mess with me again, you're dead."

"I already am," said Suzie angrily.

Rose shivered when he got in bed. "You're freezing. Mind where you put your feet."

"Have you had any weird phone calls lately?"

"No. Loft insulation ones, but nothing weird. Have you then?"

"One from someone called Isla."

"Isla? Like my sister-in-law?"

"Well obviously not her. She's been dead for years. Do you know anyone else called Isla?"

"No. That is weird. Although she was into all that supernatural, otherworldly stuff. She did come out with some strange things. If anyone was going to come back from the grave, it would be her. I know she never liked you for some reason."

"I didn't know that. You never said."

"Well, I wouldn't while she was alive, would I? I miss her. She was like a sister to me."

"Has that light been playing up?"

"Which one?"

"The big spotlight in the shed."

"How would I know? You're saying some strange things tonight, Nigel. Go to sleep."

But Nigel was having a job to sleep. He didn't believe in the supernatural and ghosts. So who was it that knew about the light? There was no one else on the road. And if there was, why had they waited all this time?

At three in the morning, at the start of the witching hour, he felt his covers being pulled slowly back off him. He almost couldn't move, but he sat up and checked if it was Rose. But she was asleep, and the covers had only been moved on his side. They were still moving. That was the moment that Nigel Knight began to believe in the supernatural.

Tuesday started with another phone call to Nigel's office. It had been Martin's idea for the supposed ghost of Isla to say something that would have been known only to one of the family.

"Martin, remember veni, vidi, *vici*."

"Who are you? If that's you, Isla, you can't hurt me now. You're dead."

"Veni, vidi, *vici*," the spectral voice repeated.

But Nigel remembered that it was one of his father-in-law's favourite sayings. He said it a lot, liking that he could speak a bit of Latin. I came, I saw, I *conquered*, thought Nigel. He always said it after they'd had a good week. But who would know that apart from one of them?

Nigel didn't know what to do. He got out his cigarettes. Rose wouldn't let him smoke in the house, not even in his office, but he didn't care. She was still on the school run. But the flame kept going out on his lighter. Almost like someone was blowing it out. Then the phone rang again. He wasn't going to answer it, but curiosity got the better of him.

"You shouldn't have smoked by the tree, Nigel."

So that was it, he thought. Someone has the cigarette ends from that night. But he had to remember dead men don't tell tales.

"Dead men tell no tales," he said aloud in case anyone was with him.

"No," said Abigail to the others. "But dead women can, can't they, Isla? And dead women can make a hell of a mess. Go on, Suzie, let him have it."

Suzie had a lot of pent-up anger. She had been killed by a car for no reason and now a whole family had lost their lives. Both by selfish people. Abigail told Hayley later that it looked like a tornado had gone through the room. Any lingering doubts of life after death had gone. Now he knew for sure that he was going to hell.

It took over a week for more calls, blood smeared on walls and lights going off and on, but Nigel was beginning to be a broken man. They'd seen him pick up his shotgun on more than one occasion and hold it to his throat. The time was right for the final part of the plan.

On the same new mobile phone that they had used to send Lady Caroline's recorded voice to Nigel, she used a local accent to ring the Gorebridge Police Station.

"I'm by the lane that leads to Red Roof Farm on the Northridge Road, and some joyriders in an expensive-looking car have gone into a hedge. If the police hurry, you might catch them."

It wasn't a coincidence that PC Bennett and PC Coult were in the vicinity and went to the farm. Nor that Rose Knight was again on the school run.

"Excuse me, sir, we're here about the car accident that happened here. Can you help us?" said Tom politely.

PC Alex Coult couldn't understand what suddenly happened. The man had collapsed on the ground and was mumbling about killing someone. He was happy they'd come and would tell them everything. He was glad he was with Tom, who got his handcuffs out and led him to the car. The man must be mad because he kept jumping as if someone was pushing him in the back. Alex told his girlfriend later that his name was Nigel

Knight and he reckoned he was surrounded by the ghosts of the family he had killed. Mad as a March hare!

Chapter 44

ON THE FOLLOWING FRIDAY MORNING, HAYLEY WENT into the library waving the latest Chiltern Weekly, until she saw someone staring at her. She let the other members of the agency look over her shoulder at the good news.

MYSTERY OF A FAMILY'S DEATH FINALLY SOLVED

Three years ago on a winter's night, Martin Fallon, his wife Isla and their two small children, James and Grace, were killed in a tragic car accident. A forty-four-year-old man has come forward to say that he was responsible. Nigel Knight of Red Roof Farm has confessed to causing the accident. He has been remanded in custody.

Detective Chief Inspector Tony Johnson told us at a news conference that it was his team that went to the farm to question Knight, and he is delighted to be able to bring closure to the most horrendous murder of an innocent family purely for monetary reasons. He hopes their family can finally move on.

"Well, Johnson got one thing right; their family can move on now," said Betty. "We spoke to Isla and they're going at last. They really want to thank you, Hayley."

"They already have, hun. I'm so pleased."

Betty added, "As Martin's dad used to say in Latin, 'Belli, billi, bolli.'"

"We sure did," said Abigail. "We came, we saw, we conquered. A very satisfying case, wasn't it?"

"He was a dead man walking once we got involved," said Lillian.

Hayley looked at Benje. "Well, I'm looking forward to having a relaxing week with my little boy. The bird table finally arrived today. You have to build it, so I might have a go at that."

"I thought you were off birds, dear."

"Well, I don't think I'll be having turkey for Christmas, but as long as they're not connected to any more murders I'm okay. And I owe it to Mr Harding."

"How is he?" asked Terry.

"He's putting all his energy into the charity shop, bless him. I don't know if the BLB club will carry on. I hope so, they did a lot of good. I might go to see if I can do anything. He apologised to me for what his son tried to do, but to be honest I feel I should apologise to him for my part in Brandon's arrest. But I suppose he was trying to kill me."

"It must have been an awful time for you, dear."

"It's still affecting me. I never used to bother locking the back door in the daytime. Now I do. I see more evil, that's for sure."

Betty said, "There's always been evil. But there are an awful lot more good people than bad, Hayley. You have to remember that."

"That's true, hun. And most of our murders happen in other villages and towns. Becklesfield is actually a very safe village to live in."

Hayley turned round to see what Abigail and the others were looking at behind her.

Two more ghosts had entered the library looking for help. Unfortunately, the young men walking towards them were covered in blood from what looked like several gunshot wounds.

"Then again," sighed Hayley. "I could be wrong! Here we go again."

THE END

Acknowledgments

A special thank you to Miika Hannila at Next Chapter Publishing.

And to Petteri Hannila for the excellent layout.

Also, many thanks to Lordan June Pinote, who has done another perfect cover.

About the Author

Ann Parker was born in Hertfordshire, England, and still lives there with her husband, Terry, and her black and white cat, Jazz.

She is the author of the bestselling Abigail Summers Cozy Mysteries – The Deadly Detective Agency, The Deadly Pub Quiz, The Deadly Regatta, The Deadly Fun Run, The Deadly Wedding, The Deadly Museum and The Deadly Coaching Inn.

Her children's stories are available in the book entitled Magic & Memories.

Ann's work is featured in magazines like Spillwords and in many anthologies, including Crime Songs, The Faintest of Tickles, Petals of Haiku and Hidden in Childhood.

When she is not writing, she loves spending time with her family, watching cricket, or reading a good whodunit.

To learn more about Ann Parker and discover more Next Chapter authors, visit our website at www.nextchapter.pub.

Publisher contact information
Next Chapter
2-5-6 SANNO
SANNO BRIDGE
143-0023 Ota-Ku
Tokyo, Japan
https://nextchapter.pub

Printed in Dunstable, United Kingdom